ONE TOUGH CHICK

ONE TOUGH CHICK

Leslie Margolis

SCHOLASTIC INC.

For Lucy,
One Tough Chiquita

ISBN 978-0-545-57276-7

12 11 10 9 8 7 6 5 4 3 2   13 14 15 16 17 18/0

Printed in the U.S.A.   40

First Scholastic printing, April 2013

Book design by Nicole Gastonguay
Typeset by Westchester Book Composition

chapter one
beware of swans . . .
and soccer players?

Saturdays are the best," I said as I stretched out on our red-and-white-checked picnic blanket, smiling and squinting up at the bright blue sky.

"You said it, sister," said Rachel.

"I must agree," said Emma. "The sky is clear. The sun is bright, and I finished all my homework on Friday night."

"And you're a master at speaking in verse," I said. "But we ended that game ten minutes ago."

Emma made an exaggerated pouty face and wiped an invisible tear from her eye. "Yes, but my brain is stuck so I'm out of luck."

I couldn't tell if she was joking or not. Rachel seemed to think not, because she whacked her on the back as if she were choking and said, "You've got to scream 'I will not rhyme' three times."

"But that is a rhyme," Emma said. "Does anyone smell lime?"

"Just do it!" Rachel ordered. "At the top of your lungs."

"I WILL NOT RHYME! I WILL NOT RHYME! I

WILL NOT RHYME!" Emma screamed so loudly my ears hurt. Then she smiled and gave us a double thumbs-up.

"Hey, it worked."

"Told you so." Rachel laughed. "And how come you can get away with doing totally dorky things like that, Em?"

"It's a gift," Emma replied, patting herself on the back with one hand. "I'm geek-tastic, and proud of it."

As Rachel and I cracked up, I checked out the remains of our lunch. All of the potato chips had disappeared—even the crumbs. The red grapes were long gone, too. As for the cheese popcorn, only a few kernels remained. The nachos and guacamole went first. And the only thing left from our peanut butter and jelly sandwiches was Rachel's crust. She never eats it. But her scrappy leftovers were nothing I wanted to snack on. I almost didn't bother looking in the cookie tin, figuring it had to be empty. But wait a second . . .

I sat up, pushed aside the paper towel lining the bottom, and found one left. Oatmeal chocolate-chip cookie perfection—score!

"Hey, look what I found. Who wants the last cookie?" I asked my friends.

"You take it, Annabelle," Emma said. "You're the one who made them."

"My mom and I ate our weight in cookie dough last night when we were baking," I said, clutching my stomach as if it still felt queasy. (It didn't anymore, but I have a good memory.)

"Yum. Cookie dough rocks," said Rachel. "I find it so much more satisfying than actual baked cookies."

"Honestly, the only reason I ever make cookies is for the dough," said Emma.

"Me, too," I said. "But you know that cliché about having too much of a good thing?"

"Did you have a cookie-dough bellyache?" asked Rachel.

I nodded, wide-eyed. "I ate so much I actually started craving salad, and that never happens. Seriously. I've had enough. So who wants it?"

Emma frowned down at the cookie. "It seems rude to take the last one."

Rachel laughed. "Okay—I totally want it, but now there's no way anyone can eat the cookie without seeming rude."

"Maybe we should split it three ways," I suggested.

Rachel, Emma, and I stared down at the cookie. It was big enough for one of us but way too small to cut into thirds.

I should've just eaten the cookie.

Not made such a big deal out of it. But now it's too late.

Of course, I'm not going to complain that my friends are all too nice. How could I, when I'm superlucky to count these girls as some of my best friends?

Rachel lives across the street. She's got dark wavy hair, a few freckles, skinny legs, knobby knees, sharp features, and a sharper personality.

Emma lives farther away, in Canyon Ranch. She's

got straight dark hair that she parts in the middle and big brown eyes. She speaks Spanish—like her parents, who are from Mexico—and French just because she wanted to learn how. Emma reads the dictionary for fun and is teaching herself physics. She's famous at Birchwood Middle School for being such a brain. No one has ever asked for her autograph or tried to sneak pictures of her with their camera phones or anything, but everyone knows she's super-smart— even the seventh and eighth graders. We're all in the sixth grade.

"Maybe we should feed the cookie to the swans," I suggested.

"Are you kidding?" Rachel asked. "I'm not getting near those things, and you shouldn't, either. Didn't you watch that video of swan attacks I forwarded you on YouTube?"

"Those were real?" I asked.

"Swans are vicious creatures," Emma said. "Last year this lady was picnicking at the park and a swan stole her sandwich, and when she tried to get it back she almost lost her finger."

"That sounds like an urban myth," I said.

"A lady loses her finger to a swan at our community lake?" asked Emma, her dark eyes twinkling with mischief. "Sounds more like a suburban myth to me."

"Except it's totally true," said Rachel. "Claire told me. Her mom was in the emergency room when it happened. She took care of the woman. Said she needed ninety-two stitches."

I looked at my hand. "How can ninety-two stitches even fit on one finger?"

"There are three different layers of skin," Emma explained. "The epidermis, the dermis, and the subcutaneous. Probably the wound was so deep the lady needed separate stitches for each of the three. It might've cut all the way through her skin and muscle to the bone. I wonder if you can stitch through muscle."

"Blech, enough! We get the picture," said Rachel.

"Crazy," I said, eyeing the swans nearby. Two of them swam in circles in the distance, totally preoccupied and ignoring us. I hoped they continued to do so.

"Hey, I keep forgetting to tell you guys," said Rachel. "I finally figured out what to do for the talent show this spring."

"Yeah?" I asked, totally curious. Auditions for the school-wide spring talent show happened on Monday. My friends and I had been trying to come up with our acts for days, and I was still stumped.

"What are you going to do?" asked Emma.

"I'm going to ride a unicycle while juggling," Rachel said proudly.

"That's amazing!" I said, truly impressed.

Emma coughed. "Um, Rachel," she said. "That does sound great, but you don't know how to ride a unicycle."

"I don't know how to juggle, either," Rachel replied. "But that doesn't mean I can't learn."

Emma and I cracked up, figuring she was kidding. Except Rachel seemed serious.

I stopped laughing. "Wait. You're going to teach yourself to juggle *and* how to ride a unicycle in four weeks?" I asked.

Rachel frowned and asked, "Yes, why? Is that not ambitious enough? You think I should add something else to my act? Like maybe I could chew gum and blow a giant bubble, too?"

"Except we can't chew gum at school," said Emma, ever the practical one.

"Have you memorized the school handbook?" asked Rachel.

"Of course," Emma replied. "But it's not like that rule is so obscure. Everyone knows about the gum."

"Don't you think they'd make an exception for the talent show?" Rachel asked.

"I don't know if gum chewing could be considered a talent," said Emma. "Not even combined with all of your other amazing feats."

Emma grinned at me, and I couldn't help but giggle. It's the way she said "amazing feats," I think.

"Stop making fun," said Rachel, throwing a handful of popcorn kernels at us. "I'm going to unicycle and I'm going to juggle and it's going to be awesome!"

"I believe you," I said, trying and failing to keep from laughing. "I'm sorry. I've just never heard someone sound so adamant about unicycling and juggling before."

"Well, what are you two doing?" Rachel asked.

Emma sat up straighter and grinned. "I'm going to speed-read," she said.

"What do you mean?" I asked.

"I'm going to read onstage for five minutes. I'm really good." Emma tucked her long dark hair behind her ears, bashful because she doesn't like to brag, even though she often has good stuff to brag about.

Excluding this particular thing, I mean. Not to be rude—I love Emma and speed-reading does sound like a cool talent. There's just one problem—it's not exactly something you can show. I didn't know how to bring up the issue without offending her, but luckily Rachel had no problem doing so. "How are you going to prove it?" she asked.

"People will see me turning pages," Emma replied matter-of-factly.

"But that doesn't mean you've actually read all the words," I pointed out. "It just shows you know how to turn pages."

"What do you mean?" Emma asked.

"She means you could fake it," Rachel said.

"I would never pretend to speed-read," said Emma, as if we'd mortally wounded her. "Anyone who knows me knows that."

"But not everyone is going to know you. There are going to be a gazillion people there," said Rachel.

"A gazillion is not even a real number," Emma said, sounding a little haughty now. "It merely represents a large number, usually used for humor or effect."

"You sound like a dictionary when you say that," I said.

"Thank you," Emma replied, totally serious.

I didn't have the heart to tell her I didn't mean it as a compliment.

"Okay, maybe there won't be a gazillion or even a million," said Rachel.

"There aren't a million people in the entire town of Westlake," Emma pointed out.

"Right, but there will be about three hundred people there, and not all of them are going to know you. And even if they did—no offense—but watching someone read onstage is not exactly, um, entertaining."

"Are we supposed to entertain, or are we supposed to demonstrate our talents?" asked Emma.

"Well, it is a talent *show*," I reasoned. "So probably, ideally, both."

Emma frowned, thinking about this for a moment. "You may have a point there. So what do you think I should do?"

"How about spelling?" I suggested. "You creamed us in Scrabble last weekend—as usual."

"I still don't know how you come up with those words," said Rachel. "Torrential. Insidious. Bombastic . . ."

"Quetense," I teased.

Emma smiled guiltily. *Quetense* was a word she made up, but everyone was afraid to challenge her on it. No one wanted to lose a turn, and no one wanted to look dumb. "Sorry about that," she said.

"Hey, babe, if you've got it, flaunt it," said Rachel. "You should totally put on a spelling bee. Maybe you can get some other kids in on the act."

Emma frowned as she pulled her hair back into a ponytail. "That sounds kind of dull."

"Then jazz it up," said Rachel. "Like, how about spelling words backward?"

"Don't you think the audience would rather Emma face forward so they could see her face?" I asked.

"I mean the words will be backward, not Emma," Rachel explained.

"I was joking," I said.

"Of course, the real problem with the talent show is that we only get five minutes to perform," said Rachel. "That's hardly enough time to do all my tricks."

"What tricks?" I asked. "You don't even know how to ride a unicycle yet."

"Or juggle," Emma added.

"I know that," said Rachel. "But I am absolutely positive that I will learn lots of tricks and that five minutes will not give me enough time in which to perform them. Anyway, isn't everyone supposed to get his or her fifteen minutes of fame?"

"Oh, right. Who said that again?" I asked.

"I did," Rachel replied. "Just now. Didn't you hear me?"

Now it was my turn to toss a handful of popcorn kernels at her, which I did happily. "I mean, who said it originally? Some famous artist, right?"

"Yes, Andy Warhol," said Emma. "He's the guy who painted thirty-two Campbell's Soup cans and called it art. He had a lot of stuff to stay about mass media and consumer culture. But I believe that quote refers to people's entire lives. Meaning they get fifteen minutes for a lifetime. So maybe it's better to use only five minutes now and save the rest for later."

"Here's a scary thought," said Rachel. "What if you use up all of your fame when you're in the sixth grade like us? Then what will you have to look forward to?"

"I don't think the universe doles out such a precise amount of fame to everyone," said Emma. "Plus, I think there are lots of things more important than fame. It's really a mixed bag. Ask anyone on a reality TV show."

"Did you see that *Real Housewives* fight last night?" asked Rachel. "I can't believe she pushed that lady into a pool."

"I think it was a fake fight," said Emma. "No way can grown-ups act that dumb."

"You have a good point," I said. "Who wants to be famous for being mean and ridiculous or for wearing super-tight, expensive clothes and having giant boobs or whatever? That seems so sad and stupid."

"Regular, non-TV people can be famous for embarrassing things, too," Rachel pointed out. "Remember when Damien farted in class? It's all anyone could talk about for weeks."

"Yeah, that was gross. I hope he didn't waste his fifteen minutes of fame on that," I said. "Poor guy."

Damien can't help being kind of dorky. The problem is he's super-pale and his black hair grows in the shape of a V. People call him Count Damula because they think he looks like Dracula, and that's not a look any sixth grader wants to sport. Not even if vampires were still trendy.

"If you could be famous for only one thing, what would it be?" asked Rachel.

"Easy," said Emma. "I'd like to be the first woman president."

"What if someone beats you to it?" I asked.

"Then I'll be the second or third woman president. That wouldn't be too terrible, either. What about you?"

"I haven't really figured it out yet," I admitted. "The problem is, I don't have any talents."

"Sure you do," said Rachel.

"What?" I asked.

"Basketball," she replied.

"That's only a hobby," I said. "And I'm good enough, but it's not like I can shoot free throws on stage."

"Why don't you dribble?" asked Rachel.

"Everyone can dribble," I said. "Even five-year-olds."

"You'll come up with something," said Emma. "What if . . . Uh-oh."

Right then Emma's mouth snapped shut and her eyes got way wide. A bunch of older boys were coming our way. There were eight of them, and they were cute, which made all three of us sit up straight and pay attention.

These boys seemed older—not much, just a little. They could've been eighth graders, except I didn't recognize any of them from school. Probably they were freshmen at Birchwood High School, unless they were in middle school like us, but went to the local private school.

Rachel, Emma, and I didn't say a word. A group of cute older boys would make us nervous anyway, but some of these boys weren't wearing their shirts—just baggy shorts and tennis shoes and socks. Some were skinny and some were regular. One had a tummy that puffed out over his elastic waistband. And one boy even had wispy dark hair on his chest by his nipples. I looked away, toward the lake, because the sight of chest hair makes me feel weird.

The boys came closer. One of them—the guy with a buzz cut and hair on his chest—held a soccer ball tucked under his arm. "Hey," he said. "You girls are sitting in the middle of our field. We need to play here. Are you done?"

"They're totally done," said the chubby guy. He spoke with authority, like he had our numbers. Not literally. I mean like he knew all about us, which couldn't have been true. Why did he think we were done?

We hadn't packed up our picnic.

We were still in the midst of a conversation.

We hadn't even put our shoes back on.

There was still a cookie in the cookie tin. How could we have been done with our picnic when there was still a cookie left? That's, like, the rule. Picnics aren't over until all the desserts are gone.

Okay, maybe it's not a rule, but it should be.

The guy with the buzz cut said, "Hey, are you going to eat that cookie?" Then he reached down and took it before anyone could answer. We all watched him, totally transfixed as he folded the entire thing into his mouth.

It seemed as if he swallowed it whole without even chewing.

He couldn't have tasted it that way.

What a waste of a cookie!

Rachel, Emma, and I looked at each other in silence, but I knew we were all thinking the same thing: *Who is this guy and why did he think it was okay to eat our last cookie?*

At least I *thought* that's what they were thinking until suddenly Rachel and Emma jumped up and Rachel actually apologized. "Oh, sorry. We're totally done so we'll get out of your way."

"We didn't know this was your space," Emma added as she scrambled to pack up our picnic, putting all the trash in a trash bag and folding up our blanket.

The two of them moved fast, like happy little soldiers, good little girls.

The whole scene annoyed me. We were having fun, and our fun wasn't over yet. So where were we supposed to hang out?

And why did we have to leave? These boys didn't

own the soccer field. Our picnic spot wasn't even an official soccer field, merely a large spot of open grass. In fact, it looked just like the large spot of open grass on the other side of the lake, which got me thinking . . .

Before I even realized what I was doing, I heard myself ask, "Do you guys really have to play here? Like right here in this exact spot?"

My friends froze, surprised. All the boys seemed shocked, too.

"We always play here on Saturday afternoons," said the one with the buzz cut. He spoke carefully, as if he were speaking to someone unfamiliar with the English language. "Ask anyone."

The only people around here were Emma and Rachel and me, plus all the guys, and obviously I already knew what they thought.

He might have been right. Maybe they did always play soccer in this spot on Saturday afternoons, but we got here first.

I couldn't help but think that if we were older, or if we were boys, they never would've asked us to leave. Something about being a bunch of young girls made them think they could push us around.

"Why can't you play over there?" I asked, pointing to the other side of the lake. "It's totally empty. And I think they just cut the grass, which means the surface will be better for soccer, right?"

He started to protest, but his chubby friend interrupted. "The girl's got a point."

"Okay, dude. Whatever." The buzz-cut boy threw the ball and a bunch of his friends went after it, like dogs chasing after a really great chew toy.

"You kids have fun," he called before taking off after them in a slow, lumbering jog.

The guy who'd stood up for me—the chubby one—had long hair and a diamond stud in his ear. "I'm impressed. You're one tough chick," he said, winking at me before running after his friends.

As soon as he was out of earshot my friends collapsed in giggles. "Go, Annabelle!" Rachel said.

Emma put out her hand for a high five. "I cannot believe you stood up to those guys."

"What?" I asked. "Just because they're older and they're boys, we're supposed to end our picnic early?"

"Obviously they didn't know whom they were dealing with," said Rachel.

"Hey, that's your talent," said Emma.

"So true." She and Rachel fist-bumped.

"What are you talking about?" I asked.

"Your talent is boy training," said Rachel. "The way you handled yourself with those guys? How you talked to them like they were anyone? It was masterful."

I blushed. I couldn't help myself. My friends were kind of right.

When I first started at Birchwood Middle School back in September I used to get picked on by lots of boys. Then I got my dog, Pepper. I read this puppy-training manual and trained my dog and discovered something cool. Dog training and people training have a lot in common.

I applied the dog-training lessons to the difficult boys in my life, and they worked.

"Okay, maybe you're right. But I don't think it would go over so well if I tried to demonstrate boy training in front of an audience. It might come across as, I don't know . . . offensive?"

"Only if people are too sensitive," said Emma. "I think you've made an important psychological discovery."

"And you can't argue with the facts," said Rachel. "Your methods work."

"Okay, but how would I even turn my techniques into a five-minute act?" I asked. "It's kind of something that has to happen spontaneously."

"How about if you pick random boys from the audience and control them?" said Emma.

"It's not like I'm a hypnotist or a puppeteer. Boy training is a subtle game. It can't be staged."

"Too true. Plus, people probably don't want to admit that their sons and brothers and whatever are as easy to train as dogs," said Rachel.

"Even if it's true?" asked Emma.

"Even though it's true, it's only true in some contexts," I said.

"But you did train Pepper," said Emma.

"I did," I said, as the full implications of her words slowly sank in. "And a puppy-training demonstration would be perfect for the talent show. Emma, you're a genius!"

I gave her a quick hug.

"If we still had the cookie, it would definitely be yours," said Rachel.

"I cannot believe he stole the last cookie," I said, crumpling up the napkin in the now empty tin.

"That's what put you over the edge, huh?" asked Emma.

"Totally," I said. "But I guess I didn't work my magic fast enough."

"Well, there's always next time," said Rachel.

"Hey, speaking of time. What time is it?" I asked.

Emma checked her phone. "Four o'clock."

"Yikes!" I jumped up. "I should probably head home."

"Oh yeah, I almost forgot," said Rachel. "You need to get ready for your big date."

"It's not a date!" I said.

"It's totally a date," said Emma.

"I'm not sure," I told her.

"Well, you'll find out soon enough," said Rachel.

chapter two
say cheese—or is that cheesy?

I hopped on my bike.

"Say hi to Oliver for us," said Emma.

Simply hearing Emma say Oliver's name made me feel all nervous and jumpy. Which is exactly how I felt about Oliver himself.

He's in the sixth grade, too. We sit next to each other in science, and we've been friends for a while. Here's what I know about him so far: He's short and sweet and cute. He's a good student, with excellent penmanship, and he loves to draw. Actually, Oliver loves all sorts of art. He takes private painting classes, and he and his parents go to museums for fun. Oliver's mom is from Jamaica, and his dad is from England. He's black and he's got a slight Jamaican-sounding accent. Oliver, I mean. His dad is white. His mom is black. And they both have accents, too. Oliver plays cricket and calls dinnertime "tea" and goes to the West Indian Day parade downtown every single year and packs Jamaican patties in his lunch sometimes.

I don't remember the exact moment I fell for him.

My crush didn't come instantaneously, like how sometimes you're stuck on one question on a test and then suddenly the answer pops into your brain—seemingly out of thin air.

I've probably always liked him on some level, but it was more of a below-the-surface type of thing, always lurking, like dust bunnies under my bed. Not to compare Oliver to dust bunnies. He's much cuter and he's never made me sneeze.

Anyway, I don't know how long Oliver has liked me. Or if he even does like me as more than a friend and a lab partner.

All I know is tonight is the night we are going out on our first official date.

I think.

I mean, I know we're going out. I'm just not 100 percent positive it's what I should call a date.

Here is what I do know:

1. Oliver and I are going out for pancakes.
2. We are going out for pancakes because Oliver invited me out for pancakes.
3. Oliver invited me in order to celebrate our team's second-place win in Birchwood Middle School's Sixth-Grade Science Fair.
4. The second-place prize was gift certificates to the International House of Pancakes.
5. Oliver did not invite our third lab partner, Tobias, because he's allergic to pancakes.

That's what Oliver told me, anyway. Which leads me to my final and most important point in regard to this matter.

6. Tobias is NOT allergic to pancakes.

I know this because I conducted an experiment last week. I sat down next to Tobias at lunch and asked if it was okay to eat a sandwich next to him.

"What do you mean?" asked Tobias, glaring at me suspiciously. "Are you going to chew with your mouth open or drool or spit your food out like some old geezer with no teeth?"

Tobias is kind of obnoxious, in case you can't tell based on the above interaction.

"Nope," I said. "And I think what you just said is offensive to old geezers. My grandma is old and her table manners are impeccable. Plus, you'd never even know she wore dentures."

Tobias scowled (he's very good at scowling) and brushed his dark brown bangs off his greasy, somewhat pimply forehead. "What's your point, Spazabelle?"

"Didn't we decide you aren't allowed to call me that anymore?" I asked, flicking his ear with my finger.

"Ow!" said Tobias.

"You totally deserved that," I replied. "I have no remorse."

"Fine," he grumbled, all sulky, frowning down at his lunch. "Now, why are you here again?"

"I want to make sure I can sit here and eat bread next to you, that you're not allergic to wheat."

"And why would I be allergic to wheat?" Tobias asked.

"I don't know. I'm just checking. Celiac disease—that's what it's called when you can't eat wheat—is very big now."

"Well, I don't have it."

"Good," I said. "Are you allergic to anything else?"

"Dust," said Tobias, rubbing his nose subconsciously. "It makes me sneeze."

"Duh—everyone is allergic to dust," I said. "I mean do you have any food allergies? Wheat, peanut butter, nuts, strawberries, pancakes—"

"Pancakes?" asked Tobias. "Are you joking?"

I shook my head no. "So you're telling me you are not and have never been allergic to pancakes, correct?"

"Are you trying to get me to fork over my gift certificate?" he asked. "Because it ain't happening. I already went to IHOP with my dad last week, and it was awesome."

It took a lot to refrain from jumping up for joy. "So you already ate your pancakes?" I asked, needing confirmation.

"Did you take a stupid pill this morning?" asked Tobias. "Because you really seem to be missing something."

I was so excited I almost kissed him. Except not really. That would be gross. And I should be careful about what I say because kissing has been on my mind a lot lately. Except not in reference to Tobias, of course.

The thing is, out of my four best friends—Rachel, Emma, Claire, and Yumi—I'm the only one of us who hasn't ever kissed a boy. And I want to—not just because my friends have kissed boys and I'm a follower. I'm not. And it's not merely because I feel a little left out, although I sometimes do feel that way, especially when they talk about kissing, which isn't that often, only sometimes, but enough. It's just I finally found a boy I want to kiss: Oliver. And I hope he wants to kiss me, too.

Anyway, instead of kissing Tobias (blech!), I gave him a goofy grin and said, "Thanks, dude."

As I was leaving, Tobias called after me, "I thought you wanted to eat your sandwich here."

"I changed my mind," I said with a wave. "See you in science."

"Whatever." Tobias turned back to his food and grumbled something about girls being weird.

Just then I thought of another point: Even if Tobias were allergic to pancakes (and maybe embarrassed to admit it to me), I am sure he would be able to find something else to eat. IHOP sells fruit and lots of breakfast meats: sausage and bacon and even turkey bacon.

As soon as I got home, I parked my bike in the garage, took off my helmet, and bounced inside, up to my room.

I turned on the Beach Boys' *Pet Sounds*. My uncle

gave it to me for Christmas. He's always giving me music: Prince, the Beatles, the Rolling Stones, Velvet Underground, the Pixies, Patti Smith, and early Madonna. Most of it's good. And it's important to him that my iPod is eclectic and contains more than the usual Top 40 stuff and random '80s hits my friends listen to. Not that there's anything wrong with that stuff, either. I love it all.

Anyway, I skipped ahead to my favorite song on the CD—"Hang on to Your Ego." The entire song seemed perfect for this situation. It made me feel so very "I'm getting ready for a big night just like a real teenager from some movie would."

Then I turned to my closet, but before I even opened it my friend Claire called.

"Great timing," I said as soon as I picked up the phone. "Oliver will be here in less than an hour and I've got no idea what to wear."

Claire is a total fashion maven, so she's the perfect person to help me with this matter. But the silence on the other end of the line reminded me that Claire also likes Oliver. At least, she used to like him. Claire and Oliver even went to the Valentine's Day dance together last month. And it was at the dance that Claire realized Oliver liked her just as a friend.

"I'm sorry, Claire. Was that super-insensitive and cruel of me to ask you for help getting ready for my date with Oliver?"

"No no no!" said Claire. "I'm just trying to picture your closet."

"Are you sure you're okay with this?" I asked.

"Totally," said Claire. "I'm calling to wish you luck tonight. It's going to be awesome, and there are no hard feelings. I promise. If I can't go out with Oliver, I want you to."

"You're the best," I said.

"I know," said Claire. "Now, tell me what you're thinking of."

I walked over to my closet and opened up the double doors. "I definitely don't want to wear jeans and a T-shirt, because he sees me in that every day at school. But I don't want to get dressed up, either, because then I'd look like I'm trying too hard."

"Why don't you wear your black miniskirt with your charcoal leggings? The leggings say, 'This is not a date,' and the skirt says, 'It's the weekend and I want to look good for myself, not necessarily for anyone else.'"

"Wow, I didn't realize my clothes could say so much," I said.

"Don't make fun—this is important!" said Claire.

"Okay," I said. "Hold on." I put the phone down and tried on the skirt and leggings. Not bad. Then I put on a gray-and-black-striped shirt to go with it. After I got back on the phone, I said, "You're right. This is perfect. I'm ready. Thanks."

"Wait!" Claire yelled. "What are you wearing on top?"

"My gray-and-black-striped T-shirt," I said. "It goes perfectly. You'd be proud."

"No, that's no good. With all that black and gray you must look like the grim reaper. And who wants to date the grim reaper?"

"Mr. Grim Reaper?" I said.

"Exactly—and that is not Oliver. Try something brighter. How about red?"

"Really?" I asked.

"Yeah, what's wrong with red?"

"Hearts are red. Lips, too."

"Yeah, and this is your first date, so red makes perfect sense. Come on—it'll be hot and you definitely want to be on fire."

"I do?" I asked. "I'm not even sure what that means, but hold on."

I searched through the laundry basket at the bottom of my closet. The clothes were all clean. My mom does my laundry but it's my job to put my stuff away. And usually I don't bother. Luckily, I found the shirt at the bottom of the pile. And Claire was right. It looked good.

"Much better," I told her when I got back on the phone. "But are you sure it's not too dressy?"

"Not at all," said Claire. "If you were going over to Rachel's to watch *Mean Girls* for the hundred and thirteenth time, you still might wear a skirt if it happened to be a Saturday night because that's the kind of girl you are."

"Good to know. Thanks," I said. "I'd better go."

"Shoes!" Claire said. "Try on those knee-length

patent-leather boots I made you get at the mall last weekend. They'll be perfect! And have fun!"

"Thanks!" I hung up, put on my boots, turned off the Beach Boys, and put on KT Tunstall's "Suddenly I See." Then I turned up the volume and bounced around my room as I brushed my hair.

Next I took out my makeup case, unzipped it, and lined up everything on my dresser. Then I realized I really needed better light for makeup application, so I put everything back in its case and carried it into the bathroom, where I unpacked it again, feeling a little silly for this rookie mistake. The entire world of makeup is new to me. Also, I'm more of an occasional traveler and I don't think I'll ever be a full-time resident.

Anyway, I have three different colors of lip gloss—pink, hot pink, and frosty pink with sparkles. My eye shadow case has twelve different shades of green, blue, violet, and gray. I also have blush, although my cheeks are fairly rosy, so I don't actually need it. It came with the eye shadow, though. Oh, and nail polish, except I never wear it because I think it looks weird and smells icky.

I brushed on some light-blue eye shadow and then applied the regular pink lip gloss, and just because I thought it would help, I used some blush. Staring at myself in the mirror, I realized three things.

One: I did not look like myself.

Two: I looked like a sunburned alien with fish lips.

And three: That was certainly not the look I wanted to be sporting tonight.

I wiped off all the makeup with a damp washcloth and looked at myself again. Now I looked human, although a little red from the face scrub.

I stared at myself in the mirror from different angles. I put my hair up and let it fall down around my shoulders again. Then I practiced smiling.

Big smile.

Little smile.

Littler smile.

Tiny smile.

Teensy-tiny smile.

Toothy smile.

Super-toothy smile that actually made me look like a scary clown.

Closemouthed Mona Lisa smile. Weirdness!

And best of all, a regular casual smile.

I think I looked good.

My hair is long and straight and blond. I have dark-brown eyes and teeth that are almost straight but not quite.

I'm skinny but not scrawny except for my knees, which are a little knobby. I'm also shorter than your average sixth grader. Then again, so is Oliver. He's taller than me but just barely.

Looking at myself in the mirror again, I decided to reapply the lip gloss. Now my shiny pale-pink lips looked nice, but were they too shiny? Did I want to draw attention to that part of my body?

Perhaps I did.

Kissing Oliver seemed like it would be fun and exciting. Kissing seemed kind of scary, too.

I locked the bathroom door and looked at myself some more. This time I puckered up my lips. They looked weird and guppylike.

I wondered if Oliver would be my first kiss. I wondered if it would happen tonight. Did I even want it to happen tonight? Is it okay to kiss on the first date? Is it okay to kiss if you don't even know if you're actually *having* a date?

I checked my watch. It was still five o'clock. How was it still five o'clock when I got home from the park at five?

Wait—the second hand on my watch looked frozen. I shook my watch and stared some more. Nothing moved. There were two possibilities.

1. Time had stopped while I'd kept moving.
2. My watch was broken.

"Honey, what time did you say Oliver was picking you up?" my mom asked.

"Six thirty," I said. "Why? What time is it?"

"Six thirty," she said.

"What?" I asked. "You're kidding. Don't say that."

"Please don't yell at me."

"I'm not yelling," I yelled. Then I added, "Sorry." I ran out of the bathroom and back into my room, flung open my closet, and tore through it again, making sure I hadn't overlooked the perfect outfit.

"You look great, Annabelle. Don't worry."

"Who said I'm worried?" I screamed. "Do I look worried?"

My mom raised her eyebrows at me, something I found irritating to a crazy degree.

"Don't ask any more questions," I yelled before she even had a chance to speak. Yes, I realized that she hadn't actually asked me anything. She'd just offered some commentary, but I didn't want to correct myself. And I blamed her for this mistake, too. My mom, who stood there smiling at me with her mouth closed, doing exactly what I'd asked her to do—nothing. Yet somehow even this annoyed me.

"And what are you wearing?" I asked.

"Yoga clothes," she replied.

For some reason I didn't want Oliver seeing my mom in yoga pants. They were just so . . . tight. And how come her hair looked so messy? Had she even brushed it today?

"When was the last time you got a haircut?" I asked.

"Annabelle, please calm down. Everything is going to be fine."

"But aren't you going to change before Oliver comes?" I asked, panicked.

"Why? I'm not going out with him. Or do you want me to come along, too?" she said, and laughed. "I haven't been to IHOP in ages."

"Not funny!" I said. Then something else occurred to me. "*Why* are you wearing yoga clothes?"

"Well, most people who wear yoga clothes do so because they're about to take a yoga class. And it turns out I'm no exception." She said it like it was the most natural thing in the world for her to go to yoga on a Saturday night, but I knew better. My mom and yoga were like oil and water. Fire and ice. Peanut butter . . . and whatever doesn't go well with peanut butter.

What doesn't go with peanut butter?

Everything tastes better with peanut butter. I quickly ran through some food options: chocolate, bread, celery, apples . . .

Cheese! Cheese and peanut butter do not go well together. My mom and yoga were like cheese and peanut butter—a disastrous combination.

"You always said you hated yoga," I said. "Something about all those people sweating and grunting in one room seemed . . . did you call it 'unsavory'?"

"I may have, but I recently realized that I've never even tried yoga."

"Did Ted talk you into this?" I asked.

My stepdad is a total fitness nut. He's been training for the LA marathon for months, and the race is only two weeks away.

"Ted has nothing to do with it," my mom insisted. "Anyway, I just came in to wish you luck."

"Luck? You think I need luck?" For some reason my voice came out in a squeaky shout.

"No, Annabelle. I shouldn't have said that. You'll be fine with or without luck. Just relax and be yourself."

My self was a nervous wreck. My hands were sweaty and my pulse raced.

Mom kissed me on the forehead before she left. "I'll see you later. Remember—your curfew is nine o'clock, and if you leave the mall, you'll have to call me."

"We're not even going to the mall!" I reminded her. "We're going to IHOP. You know that! You just made a bad joke about joining us there."

"Was the joke really that bad?" She blinked at me, a little insulted.

I threw up my hands in an exaggerated shrug. "Do I really need to answer that?"

"Oh, never mind. I don't know where my brain has been these days." My mom left me alone—finally.

I turned back to the mirror. I could hardly believe that this might very well be my first real date with my soon-to-be first boyfriend.

It made me feel mature.

Sophisticated.

Oh, and scared out of my wits.

Which is a weird expression. What is a wit, exactly?

I changed watches. Luckily, my other one—a Mickey Mouse watch my grandma got me at Disneyland—worked great.

Now that I knew it was six thirty-three and Oliver would be arriving at any moment, I didn't know what to do with myself.

Then I noticed my new camera sitting on my

bedside table. Ted had given it to me because he'd gotten a newer model. I picked it up and snapped a picture of myself in the mirror, figuring if this does turn out to be my first real date, if Oliver does turn out to be my first real boyfriend, I should document it.

When the doorbell chimed, my stomach jumped. I put my camera on my desk.

My hands shook. I clenched my fists so they'd stop, but it didn't work.

I sneaked down the hall, all the way to the head of the staircase, with my back flat against the wall, like a spy. Then I peeked around the corner. Oliver stood in the entryway with Ted, who shook his hand.

Spying on my stepdad from the top of the steps made me cringe. Ted's voice seemed too loud, his head especially bald and shiny.

I thought maybe I should remind Oliver that we weren't related by blood and he didn't even raise me or anything. I had only met Ted a year and a half ago.

Then I felt guilty because, as dorky as he is, Ted's a sweet guy. It's not his fault he's dorky. Some people are born that way, I think.

It just happens, the way some people are blond and some people are brunette. Except that's not a very good comparison because, as we learned in science, hair color has to do with genetics and dorkiness probably does not. Plus, Ted is bald.

I took a deep breath, resisted the temptation to look in the mirror again, and walked downstairs, silently reminding myself not to trip.

I smiled, while at the same time worrying that my smile seemed too big and goofy. But it turns out I didn't have to worry because Oliver cracked a goofy smile right back at me.

Also? He wore khakis and a purple shirt with a collar. My point is not that he looked super-cute, although he did. It's this: Oliver got dressed up, too.

And his hair seemed shorter. Had he gotten a haircut for our date?

Did a shirt with a collar and khaki pants and a haircut make this a date? Or simply a Saturday-night dinner between friends?

"Ready?" I asked.

"Sure thing," said Oliver. "Let's go."

"Have fun," my mom said. She must've sneaked in from the kitchen—I hadn't even seen her coming. And thankfully she'd thrown on jeans and a button-down shirt.

"Bye," I said.

As Oliver and I headed out the door all I could think was this: *It's go time!*

chapter three
the true picture

Oliver and I walked out to his mom's sleek silver sedan. He opened the door for me and I slid right in. The seats were soft and black, and the entire car smelled like new leather.

"Hi, Mrs. Banks," I said.

"Good evening, Annabelle. Normally I go by Clarice, but feel free to call me Jeeves tonight."

"Jeeves?" I asked, not getting it at first.

"Yes, I'm your chauffeur," she said with a wink. "I knew I should've worn a uniform, or at least a driving cap. It would've been much funnier that way."

Oliver rolled his eyes and groaned. Clearly I'm not the only one with embarrassing parents. This made me feel better.

"Sorry, sweetie. I should probably stay silent. Right?" asked Mrs. Banks, sneaking a peak at Oliver in the rearview mirror.

"Yeah—and try not to call me sweetie in front of Annabelle," Oliver said as he slunk down into his seat.

"Right," his mom whispered. "I suppose I should've known that." She turned on the radio, and soon we were listening to Bob Marley's "Three Little Birds." Oliver asked his mom to turn up the volume. "Of course," said Mrs. Banks. "You know I saw him play in concert back when I was a teenager in Jamaica."

"I know," Oliver said, like he'd heard her say this a million times. Maybe he had, but it's the first I'd heard of it and I couldn't help but be impressed. I don't think my mom did anything as cool as go to Bob Marley concerts. She did live in England for a while. She went there for graduate school. But it's not like she hung out with Adele or any other cool musicians.

Before we made it through the third song, we were there at IHOP.

"Shall I pick you up in an hour, or will you call me when you're ready?" Mrs. Banks asked.

"Um, I'll call you," said Oliver. Then he turned to me. "If that's okay with you."

"Sure." I shrugged. And then I worried that I shrugged too much. That maybe I should've worn an actual shrug to hide my shrugging and maybe that's why those funny shawl things are called shrugs in the first place.

We climbed out of the car and then Oliver's mom pulled away. We stood there watching from the sidewalk as the taillights got smaller and then finally disappeared into traffic. Then we walked into the restaurant.

It was crowded mostly with old people and a few families. I quickly scanned the place and didn't see anyone I knew or even anyone I recognized from school—and I couldn't decide if this was a good thing or a bad thing.

I think I'd be super-self-conscious if someone caught me on the date. But then again, I was pretty excited about being out with Oliver and I felt like a grown-up, so it would've been nice for someone to witness that. Not that I wanted to be gossiped about. Or maybe I did, as long as it wasn't for anything bad or embarrassing . . .

"Do you have a reservation?" asked the hostess, smiling down at us.

"No," I said.

"Yes," Oliver said, clearing his throat. "We do. Two for Banks." He held two fingers up in a *V* for victory.

The hostess checked her reservation book and gave a small nod. "I see—wonderful. Please follow me."

Oliver and I did. She led us to a large booth in the corner and we sat down across from each other.

And here's what happened.

I looked at Oliver.

Oliver looked at me.

We smiled and then we both looked away.

The busboy came over and brought us ice water.

Oliver took a sip of his.

Then I took a sip of mine.

Oliver reached for his glass to take another sip of water but then changed his mind and put his hand back on the table. He gripped the table's edge with both hands and then he drummed his fingers on it.

He smiled at me.

I smiled back and then felt shy and looked around.

The restaurant was loud with conversations and the clinking of glasses and silverware clanking against plates. Everyone around us seemed to be talking, yet we remained silent.

Say something, Annabelle!

I unfolded my gift certificate and put it on the table. "Think we should give this to the waiter now? Or after the check comes?"

I'm glad I broke the silence, but once my words came out I felt silly. We hadn't even ordered yet and I already seemed worried about how to pay? Not cool.

"Probably after," said Oliver.

"Right." I put the certificate away in my purse. It felt weird to carry a purse. I didn't want to, but my skirt had no pockets and I didn't want to carry my wallet around. Maybe I should've tucked it into the waistband of my leggings, though, because the purse's strap kept slipping off my shoulder. Finally, I let it rest at my side.

"Did you do the science homework?" asked Oliver.

I looked into his eyes. "I didn't think we had science homework this weekend."

"Oh yeah," said Oliver. "Um, did you do your other homework yet? Or do you wait until Sunday night?"

"Usually, I wait until Sunday night," I said.

"Me, too," said Oliver.

Silence.

It occurred to me that this was one of the first times we'd ever been alone together.

Maybe we should've invited Tobias. Sure, the guy could be annoying, but things were never quiet when he was around.

Was this what dating was about? If so, I don't know why I was so anxious to have my first one. It was kind of boring. Which wasn't fair, because Oliver is anything but boring, and I don't think I'm boring, either. Still, it was hard to know what to talk about, and both of us seemed too self-conscious to act normal.

The waiter came and welcomed us to the pancake house. He had spiky dark hair and three small hoops in his left ear and also a hoop in his nose. He seemed uncomfortable in his IHOP uniform of brown trousers with a matching vest and a white shirt underneath. I didn't blame him. I think it'll be fun to get a job once I'm a teenager, but I'd never want one that required a uniform. "Can I take your order?" he asked.

Oliver got the Swedish pancakes with bacon.

I ordered a short stack of chocolate-chip pancakes, also with a side of bacon. As soon as the waiter walked away, I worried that getting chocolate-chip pancakes might seem babyish. Also that ordering bacon seemed copycatish. Doesn't everyone like bacon? I hoped Oliver didn't think I was incapable of original thought.

"So what did you do today?" asked Oliver.

"My friends and I had a picnic over at the lake."

"Cool," said Oliver.

"It was fun," I said. "Hey, are you entering the talent show?"

"Of course," said Oliver.

"What's your talent?"

"I'm going to do some sketches. Portraits of people."

"*Portraits* as in plural?" I asked. "We only have five minutes to perform, I thought."

"I know—that's why I'm doing them fast. My act is called 'Sixty-Second Sketches.' I'm planning on doing five of them in a row."

"Can you really do a portrait in a minute?" I asked.

"Not yet, but I'm working on it," said Oliver. "Here. Let me try you." He pulled a small notebook and pencil out of his back pocket and narrowed his eyes at me. Then he started drawing.

With his pencil in his hand, he looked completely comfortable and in control, like he knew exactly what to do. I admired Oliver for having something he loved—art—and for being so good at it. I wished I had that one thing. Dog training is good, but it's not that good.

On the other hand, being drawn by Oliver and being scrutinized at IHOP made me feel uncomfortable. I worried about my lip gloss. Maybe it looked silly, and I hoped I didn't have any food on my face. Then I remembered our food hadn't even come yet. Except I hadn't brushed my teeth since this morning and there could've been food from lunch. But no—I'd spent too much time staring at myself in the mirror and practicing smiles. I knew there was no food in my teeth, and nothing else that wasn't supposed to be there. I tried to relax. Then I worried I was slouching, and slouching is a bad habit.

Turns out posing for a sketch was worse than looking in the mirror for flaws. Posing meant fearing you had flaws but not knowing what or how bad they were.

The longer Oliver's sketch took, the stranger this whole thing seemed. I felt sort of embarrassed and sort of like a model.

I wondered if models got embarrassed.

I thought about all those old-fashioned portraits I saw at my last visit to the Los Angeles County Museum of Art. My mom and Ted and I had all rented headphones for an audio tour. "Did you know that in the olden days, before photography existed, only rich people could afford to have their portraits painted? That's why, when you look at an old-fashioned portrait, all of the subjects are dressed up in fancy clothes and jewelry, sitting in fancy rooms."

"Yeah, I did," Oliver said with a grin. "And guess what else? If you wanted to be a successful portrait artist, meaning you wanted to get enough work to survive, you had to make people look better than they really were. Like, more attractive."

"Seriously?" I asked.

Oliver nodded. "Yup. Women might be drawn with finer features, and men would look more dignified, braver, stronger, maybe even taller. Children would look cuter, more playful and adorable. If they had snot on their nose, no good portrait artist would draw them with snot on their nose because they could get in big trouble with their parents. This means that all those paintings of people hanging in art galleries from way back when might not represent what people really looked like."

"So everything is fake," I said.

"Not exactly fake," said Oliver. "More like enhanced."

"The best light from the artist's point of view because the artist has complete control, right? I guess photographs are more accurate. I've been thinking about that a lot, ever since my stepdad gave me his old camera. It's really cool. I've got three different lenses. A wide angle, a zoom, and a regular lens, which also zooms in and out a little."

"You'll have to show me next time I'm at your house," said Oliver. "Except there's plenty you can do with lighting and Photoshop to make people look more attractive in photos, too."

I thought about this. "Then is it possible to portray someone accurately, like how they actually are in the world?"

"Good question," said Oliver, turning back to his drawing.

It made me wonder, am I the girl who got dressed up for tonight? Or am I really the kid in jeans from this afternoon's picnic? Maybe that's my best self because I was hanging out with my friends, relaxed and comfortable and not worried I had grease on my chin or a chocolate chip stuck between my teeth.

Since artists look at things carefully, do they see the real truth? Or a different reality? What does Oliver see in me at this moment? And does he like it?

"You seem nervous," he said, breaking me out of my thoughts.

"Huh?" I brushed my hair away from my eyes, tucked and retucked my hair behind my ears, smiled and then stopped smiling. Squirmed in my seat because I couldn't help it.

Oliver frowned ever so slightly. "Could you stop moving so much?" he asked.

"Sorry. I just don't know what I'm supposed to be doing."

I cringed, realizing that what I'd just said was way revealing. I didn't know how to pose, and I didn't know how to act on our date.

"Just stay still," Oliver said.

I tried posing as if for a photo, with my shoulders back, my chin up, and a smile frozen on my face. "Like this?" I asked.

He nodded.

My nose started itching so I scratched it. Then I crossed my legs. Suddenly my throat felt really dry, so I took a sip of water.

Oliver laughed at me and put his pencil down.

"It's really hard to stay still. Especially when I know I'm supposed to. Plus, no one's ever drawn me before."

"It's okay. I'm done. Except I think I took way more than sixty seconds. Guess I need more practice."

"Can I see?" I asked, reaching across the table for the picture.

Except I knocked over the ice water and it spilled all over his notebook.

"Yikes!" I said as Oliver kind of yelped and quickly picked up his notebook. He mopped it off with his napkin and I handed mine over, too.

Then I noticed the waiter walking by and I tapped his arm because I wanted to tell him we needed more napkins. Except he happened to be holding a tray of drinks and I must've surprised him, because as soon as I touched him he jerked back and his tray went flying.

Except this time the water didn't land on Oliver's drawing.

The water landed ALL OVER OLIVER!

chapter four
the ice (water) breaker

It would've been awesome if the sound of shattering glass jolted me out of my nightmare. If really it was still Saturday morning and I had a picnic and the date still ahead of me. But guess what? That didn't happen. I was already awake—just like the rest of the IHOP customers now staring at me, including the waiter. Actually looked down on me, both literally and figuratively, which made me feel even shrimpier and more out of place than I actually was. Something I didn't think possible.

"Did you want something?" he asked me through gritted teeth.

"Never mind," I whispered.

"Well, you've certainly got my attention now, so you may as well ask." When his nostrils flared his nose ring shifted. This made me want to scratch my nose, but I resisted because I didn't want to be so obvious.

"Um, I think we need more napkins," I said quietly.

"Right—and now you're not the only one." Just then he turned to the other tables, cupped his hands around his mouth, and announced, "It's okay, everybody; we have some glasses down but no one has been injured. Please go back to your regularly scheduled meals."

I slinked down in my seat and blinked back my tears, worried I'd get us kicked out of IHOP. Maybe I'd be banned from all of the IHOPs in America. Then I'd have to change my identity if I ever wanted to eat another Swedish-style pancake. It's either that or move to Sweden. Or maybe the powers that be at IHOP would have me banned from Sweden, too. Would a mere identity change even work? How would I get a new passport? It seemed impossible. Clearly I'd never get to eat a Swedish pancake again in my entire life.

Except wait a second—why am I so focused on Swedish pancakes? I don't even like them and hadn't ordered them.

I should be worried about Oliver. And Oliver's drawing, too. The one I so clumsily ruined. He must be so insulted. Except when I finally managed to look at him I realized Oliver was laughing. In fact, his eyes were shiny in the corners. Oliver was laughing so hard he was crying. "I know what your talent can be," he said.

"What?"

"Frustrating waiters."

"I'd say he's more than frustrated," I said, glancing back to the waiter, now huffy and talking to the host-ess. "I'd call him downright mad."

Oliver spun around and looked. "Okay, you're right." He held up his soggy portrait. "You also have a talent for ruining great works of art. Maybe we can enter the talent show together. I can draw pictures in a minute, and you can wreck them in a second."

"We'll be the dynamic duo," I said. "We already have a great track record. So can I see my portrait now?"

Oliver handed it over. The entire page was sopping wet and torn in one corner, but I could still make out the soggy drawing. A few lines placed carefully on the page had magically become a girl with pin-straight light hair and big eyes. He'd captured something true and essential, something amazingly and undeniably me. "You're incredible," I said, then immediately blushed. "I mean, this picture is incredible. I can't believe you drew it so fast."

"Problem is, it took me five minutes," said Oliver.

"Maybe you should focus on one portrait," I said.

"One portrait isn't going to win me any prizes," Oliver replied.

"Who cares? It's not all about the prize, is it?" I asked.

Oliver smiled at me. "What's it about, then?"

"I don't know." I shrugged. "It's about showing your talent . . . and having fun. How great can first prize be, anyway?"

"You're right," said Oliver. "It'll probably be a gift certificate to IHOP."

"And after showing up here with me you'll probably be banned for life," I said. "Better enjoy those Swedish pancakes while you can because they may be your last."

Oliver and I cracked up.

"So what are you doing for the talent show?" he asked.

"Dog training," I said. I started giggling, thinking about how I came up with the idea.

"What's so funny?" asked Oliver.

"Nothing." I forced myself to stop. "I'm training Pepper. I plan to, anyway."

"That sounds great," said Oliver. "What's he going to do?"

"He can already sit and shake, but I'm hoping to teach him to roll over and jump through a hoop, like in the circus."

"You think he can do all that?" asked Oliver.

"Well, he certainly likes chewing on my Hula-Hoop."

When our pancakes finally arrived we had a new waiter. This was not the most surprising thing to happen all night.

"Maybe you can set your Hula-Hoop on fire and Pepper can jump through it like dogs in the circus do," Oliver suggested.

I thought about this for a moment. "I don't think they'd let me set anything on fire in the gym."

"I know. I was kidding," said Oliver.

"Right." I grinned at him. When he smiled back my stomach flipped over.

We ate quickly.

When the check came we handed over our gift certificates. And that was it. Date over. Or was it?

"Want to go for a walk?" asked Oliver.

"Sure." I was thrilled that he'd asked, because even though our evening had started out slow (and kind of boring), I felt like we were only getting warmed up.

"Let's go," I said, sliding out of the booth.

We walked around the shopping center, standing so close to each other we brushed arms. And guess what? It didn't seem like an accident.

I saw my favorite frozen yogurt place in the distance: the Chilly Penguin. They give you a cup with dancing penguins all over it, and you get to serve yourself. They have tons of cool flavors—salty caramel, chocolate cake batter, strawberry basil, and minty mocha. Also a whole sundae bar filled with toppings.

I was going to suggest that we go, but Oliver brought it up before I had the chance. "I love that place," he said.

"Me, too. Let's go."

Suddenly he grabbed my hand, and not merely for a second, like to get me to go in a certain direction. I mean, suddenly we were holding hands.

That's when I knew for sure that we were on a date. We were holding hands and going out for frozen yogurt. This couldn't be anything but a real date.

I've never held hands with a boy before and I hoped I was doing it right. Our fingers were interwoven, and my grip was firm but not tight. The hand holding seemed determined as opposed to accidental, and I could hardly believe it was really happening. I almost wished I had my camera so I could document it, as dorky as that sounds.

Oliver dropped my hand when we got there. It happened so fast that my first time holding hands with a boy was already over. (Maybe Chilly's has a security camera and I can ask to buy the tape later. I saw that in a spy movie once.) I went to open the door, but he got there first and held it open for me.

"What are you going to get?" he asked once we were both in line.

"I love salty caramel with hot fudge but I always get that, which seems boring."

"I don't think it's boring. I think it's good to know what you want and to stick with it," Oliver said.

"I like M&M's on it, too."

"I love M&M's," said Oliver. "Know what I heard? That M&M's were invented during the war so soldiers could eat them without getting chocolate on their hands."

"I didn't know that," I said. "Which war?"

"Um, the first?" said Oliver. "Actually I made that up. I don't know which war."

When we got to the front of the line I ordered my regular old standby. Oliver chose pomegranate and blueberry swirled with gummy bears.

"Want a bite?" asked Oliver. He held a spoon of yogurt up. It had both pomegranate and blueberry and a red gummy bear on it. He'd been careful to include everything and he even gave me a *red* gummy bear, which everyone knows is the most delicious flavor of bear.

There's just one problem: I can't stand gummy bears. They remind me of cough syrup, and I don't like the way they get stuck in my molars. I took a bite anyway, and it wasn't only to be polite. It's because Oliver went to so much trouble to construct the perfect bite. And also, I wanted a taste off Oliver's spoon. Although I'd never admit that to anyone out loud. Not even to my best friends, who I knew would all be grilling me tomorrow morning. Maybe tonight. But is that weird? Not the part about keeping it private—the part about wanting it because it's Oliver's? Weird or not, it's how I felt.

The yogurt tasted delicious. The gummy bear— not so much.

I offered him a bite of mine.

He took a bite and then made a face. "I like mine better," he admitted.

"I like mine better, too," I said. "In fact, I don't really like gummy bears."

"I'm sorry," said Oliver. "You should've said something."

"Oh, I would've," I told him. "But I, um, forgot."

"Then you have to have another bite," said Oliver. "Without the bears."

"If you insist," I said, taking the spoon from him, swallowing the yogurt. "Much better! Although still not as good as the salty caramel."

"Says you." Oliver smiled.

"Hey, how come artists are always doing still-life pictures of fruit?" I asked.

Oliver paused for a few moments before answering, really thinking about my question. "I guess because fruit is easy to come by. And no two pieces are exactly alike. They're more complicated than they first appear. Like a lot of people I know."

"Really?" I asked. "Like who?"

"You," said Oliver.

"You think I'm complicated?" I asked.

"You're totally quiet a lot of the time, and I never know what you're thinking. You let me feed you a gummy bear when you don't even like them."

I smiled at him, not wanting to tell him that while I generally do not like gummy bears, I'd still wanted to try *his* gummy bear.

"See what I mean?" said Oliver. "Here you are staring at me with that cute smile, and I have no idea what you're thinking."

"I'm thinking this is fun," I said with a small shrug.

"Cool," said Oliver. "Me, too."

If eating frozen yogurt with Oliver could be this amazing, I could not even imagine how momentous kissing him would feel. But it's not like I could expect him to kiss me in a crowded frozen yogurt shop. Plus, my lips were cold. What if they turned numb? Then I wouldn't even be able to feel my first kiss.

By the time we finished our yogurt I realized we were dangerously close to my curfew. "I kind of have to be home at nine," I said.

As disappointed as I was to be ending the evening, it felt so grown-up to be complaining about my curfew. Oliver didn't need to know that this was the first and only time it had ever been instituted.

Oliver pulled his cell phone out of his back pocket and called his mom. "We're at Chilly's," he said. "No, I mean Chilly Penguin, not Chili's the restaurant. You know we went to IHOP, right?" He looked at me and rolled his eyes. "Yeah. Sure. Yeah. Mom!"

He hung up and smiled at me bashfully. "She'll be here in a few minutes."

"Great."

A parents-age couple smiled at us but we ignored them. I realized they'd probably been listening to our entire conversation. Grown-ups can be so rude sometimes—it's unbelievable!

"Let's wait outside," I said.

"Good idea," Oliver replied, already heading for the door.

Oliver's mom showed up too fast, as if she'd been waiting right around the corner. As soon as we got into her car, we stopped talking. She didn't ask us if we'd had a good time, either. She knew not to, I guess. It seemed suspicious how quiet she was. Almost as if Oliver had coached her just like I'd coached my mom and Ted.

This was good.

Oliver and I had our first date. But here I was, thinking about the date when it wasn't even over yet.

I sneaked a peak at him and, sensing the

movement, I guess, he turned to me. We smiled at each other. His eyes seemed extra green against his purple shirt, his smile extra bright. Suddenly he slid his hand over and grabbed mine. His hand was on top of mine. He gave it a squeeze but stared straight ahead, a small, closemouthed, beautiful grin on his face.

And honestly? That squeeze felt just as good as a kiss—maybe better.

We were holding hands in the back of his mom's car and it felt amazing.

When Oliver's mom pulled up to my house, she said, "Lovely seeing you, Annabelle. Don't be a stranger."

"I won't," I said, wondering if I'd answered too fast.

"Yeah, I'll call you," said Oliver.

"Sounds good. Thanks for the yogurt."

"Anytime," he said.

As I got out of the car, Mrs. Banks said, "Oliver, my sweet, why don't you walk your friend to the door."

"Mom!" said Oliver, and I couldn't tell if he was annoyed at her for calling him sweet, or for suggesting that he walk me to the door, or for simply opening her mouth. I could see getting mad at my mom for any of those offenses. Although secretly I'm glad she suggested it, because Oliver followed me out of the car and walked me to my front door.

He might have been doing it only because his mom told him to, but I didn't think so.

"So that was fun," he said.

"I know," I said. "I mean, I had a good time, too."

"Cool. Let's hang out again."

"Okay, when?" I asked quickly. "I mean, sure, if you want to. That sounds fun. Wait—you did say we should hang out again, right?"

Oliver laughed. "I did, and thanks for answering me three times."

His whole face glowed happily and expectantly in the lamplight.

I heard crickets chirp, and they seemed to be saying, "Kiss him, kiss him, kiss him" in their secret bug language.

This was truly the most romantic moment of my life. If only Oliver would kiss me! Of course, his mom was right out front. I glanced over to her. She was bent over the radio, not looking at us, so we could probably safely kiss without her even knowing it. And here we were, holding hands again. Oliver leaned closer and closed his eyes. I was about to do the same when I saw bright, blinding lights. Next we heard a rumble, and my first thought was, *Earthquake!* I should stop, drop, and roll. No, wait a second—that's for fires. What was I supposed to do in an earthquake? Stand in a door frame or run to the middle of the street, where nothing could fall on me? I couldn't remember.

But luckily there was no earthquake, just a loud rumble of the garage door because Ted was home and pulling up the driveway.

Oliver dropped my hand fast.

Ted braked and rolled down the window. "Hi, kids!" he said, before continuing on in.

"Hi, sir," Oliver called after him.

"You can call him Ted. You don't have to be so formal about it."

"Okay," said Oliver. "I'd better go now. See you soon." He turned around and jogged back to his mom's car.

Leaving me with nothing to do but walk inside.

"How was your night?" asked my mom when I walked past her. She was sitting in the living room with her knees propped up and a stack of essays at her side. Her wild blond hair was piled up on top of her head. My mom teaches high school English and usually spends weekends grading or lesson planning. Tonight was no exception.

"It looked like she was having a lovely time," said Ted, walking into the house through the garage.

"Not that you were spying or anything," I said.

"Sorry about the timing, Annabelle. I didn't mean to ruin your privacy."

"Privacy?" My mom raised her eyebrows. "Why would you need privacy, honey?"

"No comment." I sprinted up the steps before they could ask me anything else.

Once in my room I turned on my stereo and put on the Beatles' *Yellow Submarine*. Then I flopped down on my bed.

Pepper joined me and rolled onto his back. I scratched his tummy. Rachel made me promise to call her as soon as I got home, but I didn't feel like talking to anyone about my date. Not yet and maybe not ever.

I stood up and looked at myself in the mirror. Did I look different from a few hours ago? Before I'd had my first date? I couldn't stop smiling, but other than that, I couldn't tell.

I grabbed my camera and took another picture of myself.

Then I downloaded both photos on my laptop and compared my before-the-date image to my after-the-date image.

In the first photo I looked flushed and excited. In the second I seemed wiser and more experienced. Or maybe that was my eyes playing tricks on me.

Did I look older?

More experienced?

Maybe anyone else wouldn't be able to find any differences between the two photos.

Maybe I was looking too hard because it seemed like the outside of me should match my inside, and I definitely *felt* different on the inside.

Maybe it didn't matter that I didn't look any different on the outside. What's important is that I'd changed on the inside. Right?

When the phone rang moments later I picked it up on the first ring, expecting Rachel's call. I figured she'd seen me come home, since she lives just across the street and her bedroom faces my house.

Maybe she'd watched Oliver and me from her window.

Maybe she could tell me if it looked like Oliver had wanted to kiss me.

No, she probably couldn't see his face clearly from across the street in the dark.

Not unless she'd been using binoculars.

Binoculars with night vision.

Or was that creepy?

Except it wasn't Rachel on the phone or any of my other friends.

It was a woman whose voice I didn't recognize.

As I said hello, I realized Ted was on the phone, too.

"Ted? Is that you?" asked a strange woman's voice.

"Patricia, nice to hear from you," said Ted. "We need to talk."

"No kidding," she replied in a no-nonsense tone of voice.

They didn't know I was on the phone, and I hung up before they could figure it out.

Normally some random phone call for my stepdad wouldn't get me thinking twice, but for some reason, this particular one did. For one thing, it's past nine o'clock on a Saturday night, so I doubted the call was work related. And secondly, even though I didn't recognize Patricia's voice, her name sounded familiar. At first I wasn't sure why, but then it struck me.

I did know of a Patricia. She's Jason's mom. Jason is my stepbrother. He's Ted's son from his first marriage, his son with Patricia. Which means that Patricia is Ted's ex-wife.

I wondered why they needed to talk. Was

something going on with Jason? He and I are pretty close considering that we only met a year ago and he's ten years older than I am. Except he's not around these days. He's in college and living in Switzerland for the year. We e-mail sometimes, and in fact, he just wrote to me two days ago. "Hey, Annabelle—how's life in Westlake? Snow is still awesome and I'm boarding every day. Will definitely give you a lesson when I get back to town. K? Peace out!"

Jason is kind of a hippie dude, in case you couldn't tell. But my point is, if something was going on, I'm sure I'd already have known about it.

I turned on my computer and sent Jason a quick e-mail anyway. "Just embarrassed myself at IHOP, but did have some awesome froyo. See ya soon! Annabelle."

chapter five
a hot (dog) mess

When I answered the door on Monday morning I found Rachel on my front stoop with a Band-Aid on her forehead and a thick black brace wrapped around her ankle.

"What happened?" I asked.

"What happened is that I have finally perfected the art of unicycle riding," Rachel replied, dramatically holding up her new unicycle. It looked strange, like a broken bicycle with a really high seat.

I blinked at her, trying to figure out what felt off. Besides the bandages, I mean. Then it hit me. "Hey, why does your voice sound so funny?"

"Oh, my tongue is a little swollen because I bit it on my last fall," she admitted.

"Ouch!" I said, raising one hand to my own mouth.

"Don't worry," Rachel replied, seemingly unfazed. "It was totally worth it. I can ride forward and backward and turn on a dime."

"On an actual dime?" I asked.

"No, turns out that's only an expression. It means I can make super-sharp turns."

"Oh," I said. "That's still pretty cool."

"Yeah, I tried turning on an actual dime," Rachel admitted. "That's how I fell and twisted my ankle."

I shrugged. "A dime would be too small to see from the stage anyway."

"Yeah, unfortunately that only occurred to me recently, as in after my fall."

"At least you didn't break anything, right?"

"Nope," said Rachel. "And I have the emergency-room X-rays to prove it. My mom insisted that we go after I accidentally rode into our swimming pool and hit my head on the edge of the deep end. She's so over-protective."

I laughed. "It's pretty impressive that you taught yourself how to ride that thing."

Rachel and I both stared at the unicycle. "Yeah. The juggling I'm still working on. And the juggling while unicycling may not happen in time, but I figure I could do two minutes of each during my act and still have time for some jokes."

"Jokes?" I asked.

"Yup. I'm going to do a stand-up routine, too. Comedy, unicycling, and juggling. It'll probably be a Birch-wood first."

"Maybe the first in all of Westlake," I said. "I'm impressed, but are you sure you're okay?"

"Surface wounds," Rachel said with a wave of her scraped-up hand. "And totally worth it. So, are you ready?"

"Hold on. Let me get my backpack." I ducked inside

for a second to get my stuff and yell good-bye to every-one, and then I joined Rachel.

"Can I see you ride the unicycle?" I asked.

"I promised my parents I wouldn't ride it on the street," said Rachel. "Only in our backyard and onstage. But you'll see me this afternoon."

"I can't wait!" I said.

The talent show committee was holding auditions after school. Pepper and I had practiced his tricks all day on Sunday. We were ready, but I still felt super-nervous. My stomach felt so twitchy I could hardly finish my breakfast this morning, and Ted had made blueberry pancakes.

"Where's Pepper?" Rachel asked. "You're still doing the dog-training act, right?"

"I am. My mom is going to drop him off after school. It's not like I could stuff Pepper into my backpack or tie him to the bike rack."

"Good point," said Rachel.

We walked to the corner where we always wait for Yumi, but today—for the first time ever—she was waiting for us.

She wasn't merely waiting, though. She was prac-ticing her windup, pitching invisible softballs in slow motion. That's what Yumi is doing for the talent show—a pitching demonstration. Except with real balls at regular speed.

As soon as she saw us, she stopped what she was doing and said, "Hi. What took you so long?"

"We're early," said Rachel.

"I know but not early enough. It's a big day." Yumi stuffed her softball mitt into her backpack—not an easy task, since it was already filled with balls.

"How many do you have in there?" I asked.

"Ten," said Yumi. "For my ten perfect pitches. Isabella is going to catch for me, but I didn't want her to have to toss the ball back to me ten times. Otherwise my act might look like two girls playing catch."

She swung her backpack onto her back and readjusted her Dodgers cap. Her shiny black ponytail poked through the back. "Are you guys ready?"

"I am," said Rachel. "And I'm so nervous. What if I don't make it?"

"Do you really think they're going to reject people?" I asked.

"No," said Yumi. "The only reason they're holding auditions is to avoid disasters. Like last year. This eighth grader named Becky Spillman decided to do a performance-art piece involving three gallons of blue paint."

"Blue paint that splattered everywhere—including all over the first three rows of audience members," said Rachel.

"Blue paint that it turns out wasn't washable," Yumi finished.

"It was a nightmare. Everyone looked like Smurfs," said Rachel.

"That actually sounds kind of cute," I said.

"It was madness," Yumi said. "But that wasn't even the biggest disaster of last year's show. Apparently, these five eighth-grade guys decided to have a hot-dog-eating competition."

"Yuck!" I said. "Who wants to watch a bunch of guys stuffing themselves?"

"Did we already tell you about the pukefest?" asked Rachel.

"No, but I'm not sure I want to know. It's a little early in the morning to talk about puke, don't you think?"

Yumi ignored me and explained anyway. "The winner ended up in the emergency room having his stomach pumped."

"And the loser? He puked," said Rachel.

"Actually three of the losers puked," Yumi said. "Sour, pink hot-dog-flavored vomit all over the stage."

"Like I said, more information than required." I crinkled my nose.

"Two audience members puked, too," said Rachel. "After they got puked on."

"It really wasn't the year to sit in the front row," said Yumi.

"Let's not talk about puke for the rest of the walk to school, or I might lose my breakfast. Okay?" I pleaded.

My friends laughed. "We'll try to restrain ourselves," said Rachel.

We were silent for a moment, but then Yumi yelled, "PUKE!"

And Rachel screamed it, too.

I covered my ears with my hands and sang, "La-la-la," at the top of my lungs.

"Puke, puke, puke," said Yumi.

"Vomit, throw up, regurgitation," Rachel screamed.

"Upchuck!" yelled Yumi.

"Upchuck is a good one," I had to admit, dropping my hands.

"It's not just messy acts that were a problem," said Rachel. "Last year six groups danced to the same Lady Gaga song."

"Which is almost as bad as regurgitated hot dogs for some people," said Yumi.

At lunchtime, all my friends could talk about was the talent show. Claire had designed a bunch of clothes and was going to do a one-woman runway show. "My label is called Claire with a Flair," she told us. "And all of my clothes will be made out of recycled material. I have an entire tank top made out of Bazooka Bubble Gum comics, and I turned an old game of Twister into a raincoat. With the spinner on a matching hat."

"Wow!" I said.

"Except I only brought three pieces to show because I still have a lot to work on," Claire admitted.

"Want to really impress the judges?" asked Rachel. "Make something out of the cafeteria meat loaf."

Claire shuddered. "I would never even touch that stuff!"

"We know!" said Rachel.

"I'll never eat anything that can smile," Claire reminded us for the hundredth time. (She's a strict vegetarian.) "With the exception of Goldfish crackers."

* * *

By the time auditions rolled around I was a nervous wreck. My mom and I were supposed to meet in the parking lot after school for the Pepper drop-off. But ten minutes after school got out, she still wasn't there.

I watched other kids get picked up.

I said hi to Nikki, who was dressed in a purple sparkly leotard. She and Taylor and Hannah and Jesse were dancing and lip-synching to some song by Lady Gaga. I know this because they told everyone else not to perform to her music *or else*. And as far as I know, everyone in the sixth grade listened.

"Good luck," I said to Nikki.

"Thanks," she said, not wishing me luck in return. That's okay, though. I didn't need luck. I had Pepper. At least I should have Pepper.

Glancing at my watch, I realized auditions would be starting at any moment. There was still no sign of my mom but I did see Oliver.

"How come you're not in the gym?" I asked. "You are auditioning, right?"

"I am, but I forgot my lucky sketch pad," said Oliver, holding up a large notebook. "My mom just dropped it off."

Must be nice to have a mom you can depend on, I thought. Maybe my mom had a reason for not showing up. I hoped she was okay.

It's funny that Oliver and I both needed stuff for the audition. What are the odds? Okay, there's a big difference between a lucky sketchbook and a dog, and I didn't exactly forget Pepper, but still . . .

"What are you doing here?" he asked.

"My mom was supposed to drop off Pepper fifteen minutes ago. And without him I have no act."

"Why don't you call her?" he asked.

"I have no cell phone, remember?"

"Here. Borrow mine." Oliver handed over his phone. It was fancy—flat and thin—the kind you could download games and other apps onto. It didn't have a regular keypad like other phones I've used, so Oliver had to show me how to get to the numbers.

I dialed my mom's phone. It rang and rang and then it went to voice mail. I left a frantic message. "Mom? It's me, Annabelle. Where are you? Please call me at this number. It's Oliver's phone," I added, then felt embarrassed.

When I glanced over at Oliver, he bent down to tie his shoe so it wouldn't seem like he was listening. "You were supposed to bring Pepper to school. Remember? You're probably on your way and you can't talk while driving because otherwise you'll get another ticket. That's what I'm assuming. Right? So I'll see you soon . . . I hope . . ."

I hung up and handed the phone back to him. "Thanks," I said, sitting down on an empty bench.

"No problem." Oliver sat down next to me. "I'll wait with you."

"Don't you need to get in there?" I asked.

"I do, but you told your mom to call you at this number."

"Oh, right," I said. "You can leave your phone if you

want. Oh, wait. You probably don't want to do that. I'm sorry."

"No problem. I got a late audition number anyway—twenty-two." He held up his number. It was a red raffle ticket.

"I'm going right after you," I said, showing him mine—number twenty-three.

"That's so funny," said Oliver.

We were both silent, smiling at each other as if we wanted to keep talking but neither of us could figure out what to say.

"So, we should go out for pancakes again sometime, or something else. A regular dinner. It doesn't have to be breakfast for dinner. We can do dinner for dinner. Or not. I don't mind either way. I just thought . . ."

I decided to stop talking to avoid rambling, although it was a little late for that.

"Let's definitely go out again," said Oliver. "How about on Saturday night? You can come over. Or I can go to your place. Or maybe we can go to the movies. What's better for you?"

"All of the above," I said, then worried I sounded too eager. "Actually, I should check with my mom first, but I'm sure she'll be okay with it."

"Cool."

We watched the parking lot empty out.

Soon all of the buses pulled away.

"Hey, do you mind if I borrow your phone again? I'm thinking maybe I should try calling my stepdad."

"Sure." Oliver handed his phone back over.

I checked my notebook for Ted's number. I don't have it memorized because I hardly ever call him, but this was an emergency. Luckily he answered his cell phone right away.

"Do you know where my mom is?" I asked.

"Annabelle?" he replied, sounding fairly confused.

"Sorry. Yeah, Ted. It's me." I told him my mom was supposed to meet me at school with Pepper.

"That's strange—I just saw her for, um, lunch, and she never mentioned anything. When she left she said she was going grocery shopping."

"Grocery shopping?" I yelled. "Now? What about Pepper?"

"As far as I know he's still at home."

"But he's supposed to be here," I said. "It's the talent show auditions. This is my only shot."

I felt tears prick the corners of my eyes. Without Pepper I had no act. This was horrible. The worst. No—worse was that I was crying in front of Oliver. Nearly crying, that is, which is close enough.

I blinked hard and breathed in deeply through my nose. I had no Pepper, which means I had no act. How could I have no act? Everyone had an act. I had to come up with something else.

My mind raced as I tried to come up with another talent. Maybe I should do something basketball related, like shoot free throws. But that was too close to Yumi's idea to pitch strikes. Plus, there was no basket onstage. This was a disaster.

"I guess I can't be in the show," I said sadly.

This time Oliver didn't pretend not to hear me. Instead he gave me a look of true sympathy.

"Know what?" said Ted. "I'm not too far from the house. I'll run home and get Pepper."

"Really?" I asked. "That's awesome. Thanks, Ted."

"It's no trouble at all. I'm leaving right now. I'll be there in fifteen minutes."

"Okay!" I hung up and grinned at Oliver. "Ted is bringing Pepper."

Oliver smiled his fabulous, sweet, and sincere smile. "Awesome," he said.

"Thanks for waiting with me. I don't want you to miss your audition, though."

"Okay," said Oliver, standing up. "I'll see you in there. If they call your number, I'll stall them."

"Thanks," I said. "You're the best."

Oliver paused and gave me a quick hug. His shirt smelled like french fries, and I mean that in the best possible way.

"It's going to be okay," he said, his voice muffled against the sleeve of my shirt. Then he let go. "You'll do great."

"Thanks," I said.

As we stared into each other's eyes I had this funny feeling. That he wanted to kiss me. But was I supposed to keep my eyes open or closed? I squinted a bit so they were half open and half closed. It seemed as if Oliver did the same. He smiled. Then he opened his mouth and leaned forward.

This is it, I thought, *our first kiss.*

chapter six
please pass the pepper

Um, mind if I get my phone back?" Oliver whispered.

My eyes flew open. I tried to speak, but my throat went dry. I couldn't move, either. Oliver wanted his phone back. Of course that's what he wanted.

How obvious.

How embarrassing.

It took some time for my brain and body to compute this new information. This new nonkissing scenario.

"Oh, sorry. Here." I practically threw his phone at him. "Thanks so much."

"You're welcome," said Oliver. "I'm glad Ted is coming. I wish I could stay but I've got to go warm up." He smiled at me like he felt bad for having to leave me alone under such stressful circumstances. At least I hoped he felt that way.

"Good luck," I said, giving him a little wave.

"You, too."

After he took off I sat down on the bench and

waited for Ted to arrive. And, lucky for me, he made amazing time.

"Thank you, thank you, thank you!" I yelled as soon as he pulled up.

Pepper barked and jumped from the backseat of Ted's red Jeep. Once I opened the door to let him out he leaped all over me, slobbering with his wet pink tongue. "Down, boy," I said, laughing. "I'm excited to see you, too, but come on . . ."

"I got in touch with your mother and she feels terrible about this entire situation," Ted told me. "I hope you'll forgive her. She's got a lot on her mind these days."

I was annoyed, but I didn't want to talk to Ted about it. Nor did I have time.

"Are you ready for your debut?" he asked.

"Now I am."

"Good. I'm sure you'll knock 'em dead." He handed me Pepper's leash, and we ran to the gym.

It may have been my imagination, but Pepper seemed even more hyper than usual. Maybe it's because he'd never been to my school before. And he probably knew how excited I was about the talent show. I figured that meant he'd do an awesome job. He certainly had during our practice sessions yesterday.

Pepper could come, sit, stay, and speak. Not words, obviously. I mean that he could bark on command. He could also shake with both his right and his left paws, although he didn't yet recognize the commands left and right. No biggie, though, because sometimes I get them mixed up, too.

He'll occasionally jump through a Hula-Hoop, except not always on cue. I'd decided not to try that trick at school because it didn't seem worth the risk. What if Pepper messed up or simply refused to jump and the judges thought I wasn't prepared? I didn't want to blow my chances based on one trick. This audition was too important.

I figured he'd be ready for the actual show in a few weeks, but for now we'd keep things simple and not take any risks.

"You're ready to show off your stuff, right?" I asked him, once we got to the gym.

Pepper wagged his tail hard and panted, more enthusiastic than ever as we ran inside. We got plenty of attention when we burst through the doors of the gym. Everyone seemed to stare.

I looked at the three judges. Mr. Beller, my English teacher, was one of them. He's the grumpiest teacher I've ever had. He always seems tired and bored, like being at school is a chore, so this wasn't the best news.

The drama teacher, Ms. Benson, was also judging. I'd never had her as a teacher but I recognized her because she always wears a brightly colored scarf on her head, since she'd recently beaten leukemia. She'd lost all of her hair during the treatment and it hadn't grown back yet. Today's scarf was red with purple polka dots, which sounds weird but looked cool, especially with her silky black dress and gold hoop earrings.

The third teacher's name was Ms. Lerner. She taught eighth-grade math and looked young enough to be a student, almost. Lots of boys have crushes on her, I've heard, and I could see why. She's pretty, with large brown eyes and super-long blondish-brownish pin-straight hair that comes all the way to her waist. She dressed in stylish clothes—skinny jeans, tall high-heeled boots, and sparkly tops with long necklaces and bracelets that jangled when she moved.

All three judges sat at a table in front of the stage with official-looking yellow legal pads in front of them.

No one was onstage at the moment, so Pepper and I headed on over to them. "Hi," I said tentatively. "I'm Annabelle Stevens. I was supposed to audition earlier, but I had a slight problem."

"Annabelle and her furry friend," Mr. Beller said, consulting his list of names. "I believe we called your number ten minutes ago and now we're already on act number thirty-three."

"I'm so sorry!" I said. "Can you please let me go on? My mom was supposed to drop Pepper off an hour ago, but she never showed."

"What a cute puppy," Ms. Lerner said, smiling at me. "Your friend Oliver explained the situation. So we've decided that you can go on last if we still have time."

"That's great news!" I said. "Thank you so much."

Pepper sniffed at Mr. Beller's pant leg.

"Your dog is housebroken, I take it?" said Mr. Beller.

"Oh, of course," I said.

"Good. Now please go backstage so we can continue."

"Right, of course. Thank you, again." I was so grateful for getting a second shot that I practically curtsied for the judges.

"Don't thank us yet," said Mr. Beller.

"Okay, thank—I mean. Okay. Just okay."

"This better be good," he mumbled.

I felt the same way.

As Pepper and I made our way backstage, Tobias walked onto the main stage. He was dressed as a magician in a black-and-purple cape, a baggy black suit with a silver tie, and a large top hat. He carried a card table, which he set up quickly, his magic wand clutched between his teeth to free up both of his hands.

Pepper and I waited in the wings so we could watch him. I was curious because Tobias was less his goofball self and more serious than I'd ever seen him before. And his tricks were impressive.

Tobias asked Ms. Lerner to pick a card from his deck and then place it, facedown, in a random spot in the pile. He then had her shuffle the cards. When he cut the deck he revealed the card she'd chosen. Next he sawed a lady in half. Okay, the "lady" was actually a stuffed doll, but it was still cool. Then he pulled a fake bunny out of his hat. He also turned his wand into a bouquet of red and purple tulips. With each new trick he explained what he was going to do, methodically. And then, right before the magic happened, he announced, "Abracadabra, Kalamazoo, kazaam," in a booming voice, just like a real magician would.

The three judges clapped when he finished his act and I did, too. It seemed obvious that Tobias would make the cut.

"Good job," I said to him as he passed me by.

"Thanks, Spazabelle." He reached out and rubbed my head, messing up my hair and annoying me only slightly. "Hope you and Pepper don't choke."

I laughed. This was the Tobias I knew and didn't love. "Me, too," I replied.

Ms. Benson called the next number—thirty-seven. When no one showed up, she asked for the group by name. "Is Ruby Wentworth here? Ruby Wentworth, who's supposed to do some . . . Oh, dear, this can't be right. She said she's going to be sword swallowing. That must be a joke . . ."

Just then a boy jogged onto the stage. "Ruby's not here. She went home sick this morning. Sore throat."

"Not surprising," said Ms. Benson, clutching her own throat. "Poor child."

"Annabelle?" called Mr. Beller. "Why don't you take Ruby's place, since you're right here?"

"Okay," I said. "Come on, Pepper." I moved forward,

but Pepper did not. Instead he stared at the ground with this strangely blank expression in his eyes. "Let's go, buddy," I tried again, tugging at his leash.

Pepper whimpered and rested his head on his front paws.

Uh-oh.

"This is no time for you to get stage fright, buddy. Come on, Pep. We've got to go." I tugged on his leash again—not too hard because I didn't want to hurt him. But he had to know I meant business.

"Annabelle?" called Ms. Benson. "Is everything all right?"

"Yes, of course," I said. "Pepper's just . . . Well, I don't know what Pepper is doing. He's never acted like this before, but we'll be there in a second." I bent down and scratched Pepper behind his ears. "Come on, guy. We've got to get out there onstage so you can do your thing, okay? It'll be fun. I'll give you a cookie after."

Pepper's ears pricked up at the mention of a cookie and he finally stood.

Once we got onstage Ms. Lerner said, "Please introduce yourself and tell us about your act."

I squinted out at the judges and the otherwise empty auditorium.

"I'm Annabelle Stevens and this is my dog, Pepper," I said. "I'm his trainer, and we're going to do some tricks."

I dropped Pepper's leash and commanded him to sit.

And that was my first mistake.

Pepper did not sit.

Pepper did the opposite of sitting.

Pepper sprang into action. In other words—he ran away.

Head bent in concentration, back arched, and legs moving so fast they blurred, Pepper galloped offstage like a racehorse.

"Pepper, wait!" I yelled, but he didn't hear me, or at least he didn't acknowledge me. I have never seen my dog move so fast.

Seconds later I heard the crash of cymbals.

When I got close, I found Hunter Miller on the ground. Pepper had crashed into his one-man band.

"Sorry!" I said, chasing after Pepper and tripping on his drum. "Sorry again." I went for Pepper's leash, but he was too fast for me.

Soon he darted under a table, out of sight. "Dog on the loose!" someone shouted.

For some reason, a bunch of kids backstage started yelling—as if Pepper were some sort of monster and not an overly excited mutt.

And the noise just got him more riled up. I couldn't see Pepper anymore, but I could hear him barking frantically.

"Where is he?" I asked, tearing through the crowd, surprised by how many kids were backstage.

I saw singers in sequins and some pirates of the Caribbean. One of them looked just like Johnny Depp's character from the movie, with thick black eyeliner, a ruffled shirt, and everything. There was also a barber-shop quartet and one eighth-grade baker whose name I didn't know, glaring at me and obviously thinking thoughts I didn't want to hear. Before I passed him by he stopped me in my tracks.

"Your dog just ate my key lime pie," he said, pulling his tall white chef's hat straight.

"Pepper ate a pie?" I asked.

"Yes," said the baker. "And I am not amused."

"Um, neither am I." I gulped an apology before turning away.

Meanwhile, someone from the string quartet was in the middle of a sneezing fit. "Will you get that thing out of here? I'm allergic."

"He's not a thing," I said, insulted. "He's a dog. And do you know where he is?"

The baker did not know and neither did the singers or the string players. I searched the area for a friend or even simply an acquaintance—but I couldn't find a soul to help me catch Pepper. And soon his barks faded, leaving me with no idea of where my dog had disappeared to. Until suddenly a familiar scream from the main stage answered my question.

I ran onto the stage to find Pepper tangled with Taylor's dance crew. Taylor was on the ground with Nikki, Hannah, and Jesse all huddled around her.

Finally Pepper ran up to me and jumped, licking my face, joyously and completely oblivious to all the chaos he'd caused. "What happened?" I asked.

"Your dumb dog knocked me over and put a run

in my stockings," said Taylor as she got to her feet. She turned toward the judges. "That's not fair. We need another shot."

"Of course," said Ms. Benson. "Whenever you're ready."

Suddenly Pepper sat down and offered me his paw. I kneeled in front of him and scratched him behind the ears. "You okay, buddy?" I asked. And then I looked at Ms. Benson, Mr. Beller, and Ms. Lerner.

"I guess there's no point in me asking for another shot, too, huh?" I asked. "Because Pepper seems much calmer now. I'm sure he'll do great."

It was true, too. Now that Pepper had finished his freak-out moment he sat at my feet, totally relaxed, friendly, and obedient.

As his tail wagged the judges looked at each other. Then Mr. Beller cleared his throat. "I think it's time for you and your dog to go home now, Annabelle."

chapter seven
the official cut

It couldn't have been that bad," Oliver said, trying to reassure me on the phone later that night.

"No, it was worse than bad," I said. "You didn't see."

"I know, but I heard it was pretty wild."

"You heard?" I cringed. "From whom?"

"From everyone," Oliver said.

"Everyone? Um, what's the opposite of reassuring?"

Oliver laughed. "Sorry. Not everyone. Just a few people. Tobias told me first. And honestly? He seemed way impressed that you could cause that much chaos so quickly. And Fred. He was, well . . . *impressed* wouldn't be the right word."

"Fred? I don't even know anyone named Fred."

"Maybe not, but your dog is very familiar with his key lime pie."

"Oh, Fred, the baker," I said. "You know that guy? I can still picture his fuming face. Good to know I have enemies I can't even name."

Oliver laughed. "It's not so bad. Plus, now you can name him."

"Ha! Here I am laughing while my dog is ruining my life! I should've known he'd freak out at school."

"How could you have known that?" asked Oliver.

"I don't know. I'm just so upset that I can't be in the talent show anymore. Everyone is in the talent show."

"The final list isn't even up yet. And you have lots of talent. You don't need to prove it."

"That's sweet of you to say."

"I'm not saying it to be sweet. I'm saying it to be honest," Oliver replied matter-of-factly. "Who beat me at hoops the other day?"

"I did," I said, smiling. "But basketball isn't a talent. It's not like I'll ever play for the WNBA."

"You don't know that," said Oliver. "Now, what did you get for number six?"

"Thirty-seven," I replied.

"Good. Me, too."

Oliver and I were doing our math homework together, since we had the same teacher. Our classes met at different times but the homework was always the same. And he'd called me a little while ago asking for help.

I suddenly heard a knock on the door. It was my mom, whom I hadn't seen since the Pepper freak-out incident. But wait—let me be more specific: I hadn't *wanted* to see her and I still didn't.

She came into my room and flashed me a sheepish smile as she sat down on my bed.

I groaned and said to Oliver, "I've got to go."

"Okay, see you tomorrow," he said.

"Bye."

As soon as I hung up my mom launched into a gushy and much-too-late apology. "I'm so sorry about Pepper, sweetie."

"What happened?" I asked. "Where were you?"

"I'm sorry. It's embarrassing, but I simply forgot. I don't know where my head is these days. I knew I had to bring you Pepper this morning. I even put some dog treats in my purse. I was running errands, and the entire thing slipped my mind."

The way she said "slipped her mind" made me think of someone falling on a banana peel. Which made me think of clowns and how clowning was one of the talents of this group of seventh-grade boys. And how everyone has a cool act for the talent show except for me.

It didn't make total sense, but I felt like if my mom had brought Pepper to school when she was supposed to, if he'd had time to get used to all the sights and sounds and smells, and if I hadn't rushed him to the stage, well then maybe things wouldn't have gone haywire.

And I was not about to let my mom off the hook so easily. "I can't believe you forgot something so important."

"I know. I'll make it up to you, okay?"

"Really? Will you build a time machine so we can go back to this morning and start over? Because that's the only way to make it up to me," I huffed.

"I was thinking more like maybe we can get some

frozen yogurt or go on a hike this weekend. Unless you'd rather go to the beach."

"Frozen yogurt is not going to get me into the talent show," I informed her. "But I guess we might as well go for that hike, since I'll have plenty of free time this weekend."

"Good," my mom said brightly.

"Since I'll be the only one of my friends not working on my talent," I added, taking pleasure in watching her smile droop.

I pulled my knees up to my chest and crossed my arms over them. Pepper lay next to me—perfectly calm and sweet.

"I'm so sorry, Annabelle. I realize how disappointing this all is and I wish I could change things. I would if I could," my mom replied. "I haven't been feeling like myself lately."

"Whom have you been feeling like?"

"Annabelle, please . . ."

"Oh, wait, I know. You've been feeling like someone who'd let down her only daughter."

"Ouch," said my mom. "I'm going to leave you to finish your homework. I don't need to take any more abuse. Okay?" She kissed the top of my head. She meant it to be comforting but instead it made me feel like a baby.

As soon as she left the room the phone rang, and this time it was Rachel. "Did you see the website?" she asked without even saying hello.

"What website?" I wondered.

"The list of talent show participants is posted on the school's website. I made it even though I fell off my unicycle and dropped my juggling balls. I guess I exaggerated a bit when I said I'd *perfected* unicycling. But obviously they can tell I have a lot of potential."

"That's awesome. Congrats," I said. I headed to my computer feeling hopeful. If Rachel had flubbed her act and still gotten in, maybe just showing up with Pepper would be enough to qualify . . .

I pulled up the list and searched for my name. The participants were broken down by grades, and I couldn't find mine on the sixth-grade list. I checked the seventh- and eighth-grade lists just in case a mistake had been made, but unfortunately it hadn't.

"I'm not there," I said.

"But everyone's there," said Rachel. "How is that possible?"

"You didn't hear?" I asked.

"Hear what? I had to rush to the dentist right after my audition and I just got home," said Rachel. "You're the first person I've spoken to since I got my braces tightened."

I took a deep breath and told her the whole crazy story.

chapter eight
he let her eat cake

Annabelle! How are you?" Claire asked me at lunch the next day. "I'm so sorry about the Pepper mess. It stinks that they didn't give you another audition. It's so not fair. And I was thinking—do you want to help me with my fashion show? Because I could totally use a partner. My line is already called Claire with a Flair, but I'm sure we can come up with a way to use your name, too. Annabelle and Claire with a Flair? Or maybe that's too long."

Claire chewed on a carrot stick as she contemplated. "How about A&C Designs? That sounds cool, except I think there's already a line called C&C and I don't want us to get in trouble for copyright infringement."

I didn't actually know what copyright infringement was, but that wasn't really the issue. Claire was a good friend and she was only trying to help. This I knew. But the entire thing made me feel worse.

"I don't really know anything about fashion, remember?" I asked. "I can hardly get dressed without you. Plus, I can't even sew a button on straight, so I think you'd be better off without me."

"Are you sure?" asked Claire.

I nodded. "I'll be fine," I said. "It's just one talent show. Not a big deal at all." I wish I believed those words myself.

Emma and Yumi glanced at each other, worried, like they didn't know what to say. I hadn't seen their auditions, but they must've gone well because they made the list, too. All of my friends had.

Rachel showed up late to lunch with flushed cheeks and juicy gossip.

I can always tell when Rachel is super-excited about some news because her face turns red and she starts talking faster and faster. She's the human equivalent of a windup toy—except she doesn't run out of juice. Ever.

It's all *chatter, chatter, chatter, chatter, chatter*—nonstop.

At least it seems that way.

And, of course, today's gossip was all about the talent show. I'd never escape it!

"Taylor kicked Nikki and Jesse out of her act because when Jesse moved her lips during the chorus she looked like a fish," Rachel said.

"That's so mean!" said Yumi. "Is it true?"

"Kind of," said Rachel. "And also she didn't dance well enough."

"Taylor is so terrible," said Emma. "But why did she have to kick out Nikki, too? I thought they were best buds."

"They are, or at least they were, but then Nikki

defended Jesse and Taylor got mad," said Rachel. "Although honestly I think Taylor was worried about Nikki being too good and making her look bad. So the whole 'siding with Jesse over her' is probably just a convenient excuse."

"So Nikki and Jesse are out of the talent show?" Claire asked, elbowing me. "See, Annabelle. You're not the only one."

"No, they're still in it, but now they've formed their own group," said Rachel. "And both groups are fighting because they want to dance to the same Lady Gaga song. Mr. Beller says if one group doesn't volunteer to use a different song, then neither will get to use it, which is just making them fight more."

We all glanced toward Taylor's regular lunch table. She and Hannah were eating in silence and Nikki and Jesse were nowhere to be seen.

"Banished from the table," Rachel whispered conspiratorially. "It must be bad."

"What a mess," said Yumi. "Huh, Annabelle?"

"What?" I asked.

"Are you okay?" Rachel asked.

My friends all looked at me with sympathy. I could hardly stand it. "I'm fine," I said. "It's not a big deal. It's just one stupid talent show. And it's not like I need to prove my talent to the world. It's kind of show-offy, don't you think?"

Everyone stared at me with hurt expressions on their faces. I'd somehow managed to insult all of my friends in one fell swoop.

"I'm sorry," I said. "I shouldn't call it stupid. I guess I need more time to get over it."

"I get it. The wound is still fresh. We can talk about something else," said Claire.

"Did you hear about that eighth grader who's in the hospital for trying to swallow a sword?" asked Rachel.

"Rachel!" I yelled.

"What?" she asked.

"I thought we weren't talking about the talent show."

"I'm not," said Rachel. Suddenly her eyes got wide. "Wait, you mean she was sword swallowing as a talent?"

"No." I laughed. "She got super-hungry and decided that a ham sandwich wasn't going to cut it."

"Cut," said Yumi, clutching her own throat. "Ouch."

No one knew what to say after that, so we ate the rest of our lunch in silence.

I went straight home after school that day even though Rachel and Yumi had plans to make smoothies and short sheet Jackson's bed. It sounded fun, but I didn't want to get stuck talking about the talent show the whole time, and I didn't want them to feel awkward, like they couldn't mention it around me, because obviously it's all they wanted to talk about.

When I got home from school that day I heard voices from the kitchen. This was strange because normally no one is home when I get in.

And another weird thing? I smelled cake. Ted is an awesome baker. I ran inside and called, "Hi, Mom. Hey, Ted. Is that a cake I smell?"

I skidded to a stop because my mom? She wasn't in the kitchen.

Ted was there with another woman!

She had frosted-blond hair with dark-brown roots. She wore bright red lipstick and a tight lavender dress, shiny black high heels on her feet and shimmery stockings on her long legs. Sitting on the chair next to her was a giant patent leather purse that matched her shoes. All I could think was, *Fancy, fancy, fancy.* That purse was too fancy for our floor. It needed its own chair.

For a moment we stood there staring at each other.

I was trying to figure out what was going on. She seemed as surprised to see me as I was to see her. Something in the look in her eye—or maybe it was the shape of her jaw—seemed vaguely familiar. Her large dark eyes, too. I just couldn't tell why.

"Um, hi," I said, because what else do you say when you walk in on your stepdad with another woman? I mean, yes, they were just sitting in the kitchen drinking tea, but still, why were they sitting in the kitchen drinking tea on a weekday afternoon?

And how come she was using my mom's favorite cup? It's blue and it has flowers on it. It was my great-grandmother's. I never knew my great-grandmother. She died before I was born. But she and my mom were super-close. I'm actually named after her. Well, her name was Anna Marie. My mom took the first half of her name and added the *belle*.

The fact that this woman used Anna Marie's cup didn't sit right with me.

"Hi, Annabelle. How was school?" asked Ted, as if the scene in our kitchen was completely normal. He was dressed in a suit—like he always wears to work, but his red tie hung loose around his collar and he wasn't wearing shoes. Ted never wears shoes in the house, which is normally no big deal, but seeing him in his socks with this woman seemed wrong, too intimate somehow. Especially since he had a hole in one toe. Who was Ted exposing his big toe to, anyway?

"Fine." I looked away and felt like disappearing.

"Can I cut you a piece of cake?" asked Ted.

"Um, no thanks," I said, thinking no way am I going to eat cake in front of this strange woman. Ted saw me looking at his friend, or whatever, and he smiled.

"I'm sorry. I forgot that you two have never met. Annabelle, this is Jason's mother, Patricia."

"Oh, hi," I said—not saying what I was really thinking, which is this: *That's why she looked so familiar. She's the mother of Ted's son.* In other words—this is the woman Ted was married to before my mom.

That meant Ted and his ex-wife were having cake together. I breathed a sigh of relief. And this was immediately followed by a bout of panic because wait a second . . . What was she doing here? And *why* were they having cake together?

As far as I knew, Ted and Patricia got divorced ages

ago and they'd never hung out before. Yet she'd called here the other night and now they were spending a lot of time together. Were they getting back together? What would I do if they were getting back together? Why else would they be here eating cake?

And not just any cake but vanilla cake with pink frosting and not just on top. This cake had three layers. Like it was Valentine's Day or something. Why were they eating Valentine's Day cake?

I guess Patricia saw me staring at her plate because she said, "Would you like a slice, Annabelle? Ted is a wonderful baker, but I guess you know that."

"I do," I said.

She smiled at Ted. "I miss your baking."

"Sweet of you to say," said Ted.

"Where's my mom?" I asked pointedly.

"Oh, she's out," said Ted. "She had some errands to run."

I couldn't believe my mom was out running errands while Ted was hanging out at our house with his ex-wife. I wanted to ask if she knew about this reunion, or whatever it was, but I felt too awkward to do so. Anyway, what if the answer was something I didn't want to hear?

Because it's entirely possible that she didn't know. That they were meeting in secret.

"I'm going upstairs," I said, hurrying off, since sticking around seemed unbearable.

Pepper and I played fetch in my room for a little while and then I put away my tennis ball and tried to focus on my homework. Unfortunately, there was too much going on to focus on English homework, so I called Oliver instead.

"Hey!" I said. "What's up?"

"Not much. I'm trying to finish some homework before my art class tonight."

"Cool," I said, thinking about Ted and Patricia downstairs. I could hear her laugh. She sounded kind of like Jason. This made me almost like her, but also not. I should've stayed downstairs, pulled up a chair, reminded Ted that he had a new family now. Defended my poor mom, who wasn't even around to defend herself.

Patricia's heels must have been five inches tall. My mother never wore heels.

"Are you okay?" asked Oliver.

"Huh?" I asked. "Yeah, I'm fine. I'm sorry I'm kind of distracted. Something weird happened."

"What?" asked Oliver.

"Well, not totally weird. Just a little. And maybe it's nothing," I replied feebly. "Actually, I don't know what it is."

"I'm confused," said Oliver.

"Me, too. I came home and found my stepdad having cake with his ex-wife," I said.

Oliver was silent at the other end of the line. "What kind of cake?" he asked eventually.

"Vanilla with pink frosting. In our kitchen! And she's dressed up all fancy, in shimmery stockings and tons of makeup, and she told Ted she missed his baking."

"Whoa. Do you think your mom knows about it?" asked Oliver.

"I don't know."

"Are you going to tell her?" he asked.

"I should, right?"

"Probably. Or you could ask Ted what she's doing there."

"Just ask him?"

"Sure," said Oliver. "Why not?"

It seemed so simple—too simple. "Maybe," I said. "I should go."

"Okay, see you later," said Oliver.

"Bye," I said, hanging up.

When I got downstairs Patricia was gone and Ted was in the kitchen cutting up vegetables for a salad.

"Where's your . . . um . . . where's Jason's mom?" I asked.

"Oh, she left a while ago," said Ted. "Want to peel some carrots?"

"Sure."

He handed me the peeler, and we worked side by side in silence. Oliver was right—I should ask Ted what Patricia was doing in our kitchen. And part of me wanted to but apparently not the part of me that actually controls my mouth, because I didn't say a word.

If Ted was going to leave us for Patricia, he wouldn't have been out in the open about it, right?

Did people leave their wives for their exes?

Why would they have gotten divorced in the first place?

She didn't seem anything like my mom. She had long fake nails. Her eyelashes were coated in mascara. My mom is a simple eye shadow and neutral lipstick kind of gal.

And right as I was thinking that, my mom walked through the door, loaded down with shopping bags.

"You need help?" asked Ted.

"No, this is everything," said my mom.

"What did you get?" I asked.

"New jeans," she replied. "My old ones were getting a bit snug."

She and Ted shared a smile. Then she walked up to him and kissed him on the lips.

"How was your day?" she asked.

Ted looked at me and smiled. "It was fine," he said.

He didn't mention Patricia in that moment or for the rest of the night, which seemed like a bad sign.

But even worse than that, I didn't mention her, either.

chapter nine
it's electric!

Mr. Beller asked me to stay after class on Friday, and I figured he was going to scold me for Pepper's behavior, which is not something I was exactly surprised or excited about. I just hoped I didn't get detention or anything because it wasn't my fault my dog acted crazy.

Maybe I should tell him about how Pepper didn't have time to warm up, and how I'd had no idea he'd get stage fright. Would he be sympathetic? It's hard to tell. I didn't think Mr. Beller was a dog person. He seemed too fussy. He didn't seem like a cat person or a hamster person, either. Cute furry animals were probably not his thing. Goldfish seemed too friendly, and I couldn't imagine him taking care of a frog or a turtle. Probably, he was more into cacti. The dry, prickly plant certainly fit his personality.

This is what I was thinking as I walked to his desk, my shoulders already slumped in disappointment and embarrassment.

Mr. Beller wore his usual surly expression. Even his voice sounds surly. If he were a woman he'd be named Shirley, and everyone would call him Surly Shirley, except only behind his back.

"How's your dog?" Mr. Beller asked.

I cringed. "He's fine, now, totally back to normal. And he's never behaved that way before. I'm so sorry. If I had any idea that Pepper would spaz out like that, I never would've brought him to school."

Mr. Beller's features twisted up into a funny expression—one I'd never seen before; one that seemed the opposite of surly.

Then he really surprised me. My cranky English teacher? He let out a huge belly laugh.

"You should've seen the faces on those girls in the dance troop when Pepper came running. You'd have thought they were being attacked by an army of hungry polar bears. It was hilarious!"

His eyes got squinty and his face turned red and his whole body trembled as he tried to contain his laughter. Soon he was giggling but clearly trying not to. He reminded me of a stout teakettle about to boil over.

It seemed kind of mean to laugh at Taylor and her crew, but if I removed my personal stakes from the situation I had to admit—it was probably funny seeing them scramble.

Was this why Mr. Beller asked me to stay after class? So we could laugh together?

It was odd, but at the same time nice. Certainly a relief, and how cool to see a different side of him.

"Is that all?" I asked.

"No," said Mr. Beller. "Sorry. I just—no, I can't help it." He let out another laugh and then coughed a few times, and suddenly he was back to his usual self. "Okay, so I was talking to the talent show committee, and we've decided to try something new this year. Shake things up a bit with some student judges."

"Student judges?" I repeated. This sounded interesting.

"Yes. We're going to select one student from each grade to participate in the judging process. We figure you're responsible enough. Some of you, anyway. And who better to judge students than other students? Of course, this could turn out to be a disaster. We'll see. We're willing to take that risk. Or at least Ms. Benson and Ms. Lerner are willing, and I was overruled. So what do you think?"

"I think it sounds great. Um, who's responsible for selecting these student judges?"

"Ms. Lerner, Ms. Benson, and myself. And we already have. Annabelle—it's you. If you're interested in the job."

"You're asking me if I want to be a judge?" I needed to confirm before I got too excited.

Mr. Beller nodded only once, as if he wasn't quite committed to the idea. "If you want to. You don't have to at all. Please don't feel that just because I've asked you means I think you—"

I jumped up and down. "Are you kidding? I'd love to judge the talent show! That sounds amazing, and I bet I'll be good at it, too. I watched a ton of reality TV over winter break. Five episodes of *The People's Court* alone."

"Let's not get carried away. I said you'll be *one* of the judges," Mr. Beller told me. "The sixth-grade judge."

"Right," I said, nodding with excitement. "I know how it works. We'll all be a panel, like on *American Idol* . . ."

"Yes, but with less commentary and hopefully no controversy," Mr. Beller replied.

"That is so unbelievably awesome!"

"So shall I take that as a yes?" asked Mr. Beller.

"Nope," I replied. "Take it as a definite!"

The students from Mr. Beller's next class were filing into the room, and he told me I'd better head out myself because he wasn't about to write me a tardy slip.

"Okay, thanks, Mr. Beller."

"You're welcome, Annabelle. I'm sure you'll do an adequate job."

"Oh, I will," I promised, hurrying out the door.

I couldn't wait to get to lunch so I could tell my friends the great news. Me, a judge. Judge Annabelle deciding who's going to go home a winner and who's going to just go home, to paraphrase that *Project Runway* lady.

Oh, what power. Yippee!!!

When I went to get my lunch, I found Oliver leaning against my locker. His arms were crossed over his chest and he was clearly waiting for me. Also? He looked cute, cute, cute, like always.

"Hi," I said.

Oliver grinned. "You're in a good mood," he said.

"I am," I replied.

"Does this mean you're feeling better about the whole talent show thing?"

"Yup. I'm fine. Pepper's fine, too. Not that he ever cared. My point is, we're all great. And it's funny you should bring up the talent show, because guess what?" I told him all about my conversation with Mr. Beller.

"Wait, you get to judge the show?" he asked.

"I get to be one of the judges," I said. "The only sixth-grade judge, but there's a big panel. Six of us, I guess. So I'm only one-sixth of the deciding factor."

Even with downplaying the whole thing I knew it still sounded pretty cool.

"That's amazing!" Oliver held out his fist and we fist-bumped. "Way to go, Annabelle."

"I know, right?"

"I'm so lucky," Oliver said.

"Right. Hold on. What do you mean you're so lucky?" I asked.

"Well, you know," said Oliver. "If you're judging, that means I have a great shot at winning."

I tilted my head to one side and studied his smiling face. "Why would it mean that?" I asked.

"Because my girlfriend is one of the judges," Oliver replied.

"Wait, what?" I asked, confused and wondering if Oliver could possibly be talking about one of the seventh- or eighth-grade judges.

Who were those girls, anyway?

But—Oliver didn't even know there were student judges. Unless he was only pretending to act surprised when I told him. But Oliver wouldn't do that. He's a very honest and genuine guy. There's not a phony bone in his body . . . I don't think.

So that could mean . . . Or it could mean . . . Might he be talking about me? I was afraid to think it and afraid to hope it.

I was so nervous and excited and freaked out I could barely look at Oliver, but once our eyes met he said, "You heard me."

"Did you just call me your girlfriend?" I asked.

"Yeah, but I guess I'm getting ahead of myself. What I should've said, I mean what I should've asked you was, do you want to be?"

"You mean, do I want to go out with you?" I asked.

"Yup." Oliver nodded. "So do you?"

"Yes," I practically shouted. "I mean yes. Sure. That sounds fine. Nice. Great." I tried to reply in a slightly more subdued tone of voice, but my enthusiasm couldn't be contained.

Not when I felt like doing backflips.

Metaphorically speaking, of course. I can't do a real backflip. If I tried, I'd probably crack my head open, and how happy could I be with a broken head? Not very. It would totally ruin the moment.

"Cool." He smiled at me—dazzling white teeth, bright green eyes, beautiful brown skin.

I realized something then, staring at Oliver with

the crowd of kids rushing past us on their way to lunch. Now that we were going out we probably would kiss.

This was good because Oliver's lips were so, well, kissable. Full. A little moist and not at all chapped. Except I had to control myself. We only just officially started going out ten seconds ago. There wasn't any need to rush things. Plus, we were in the middle of school. I didn't even want him to know I was thinking about kissing.

"Well, I'd better get to lunch now. My friends are waiting," I said.

Oliver offered me his fist and we fist-bumped again.

Would it be crazy to say that when our knuckles touched I felt a magical, spine-tingling electric charge?

One that promised kisses in the future?

Maybe so, but it's the total truth.

chapter ten
the kissing club

I tried to be cool about this news, but as soon as I got to lunch I had to tell my friends. And luckily, everyone was already there by the time I made it to our table. I looked around to make sure no one was eavesdropping on us. No one seemed to be, but I lowered my voice anyway, just in case. "Guess what? I'm going out with Oliver."

"Yes!" Rachel cheered.

Yumi gave me a high five.

Emma flashed me the sweetest smile and said, "Awesome."

And Claire broke out into a huge grin. "That's amazing!" she said.

She seemed sincere, but I had to double-check. "Are you sure?" I asked.

"Positive!" said Claire. "Why wouldn't I be?" She looked me straight in the eye, which made me squirm in my seat.

"Well, you used to like him and—"

"And my crush on Oliver is old news. I'm happy for

you. I mean, obviously I wish I could go out with Oliver myself. But if I can't have him, you should."

Claire brushed her bright red hair off her shoulder and then leaned in to give me a quick hug. "Anyway, this is hardly shocking. You guys were already dating."

"We went on one date," I said.

"One for now," said Claire, smiling wide. "But soon there'll be more."

"So has he kissed you?" Rachel asked.

I laughed. "No! We've only been together for ten minutes."

"Well, what are you waiting for?" asked Yumi.

My friends all giggled.

"Will you please keep your voices down? I don't want to talk about kissing at school."

"Annabelle's going to have her first kiss," said Emma, ignoring my request. "That's so fierce."

"Welcome to the club," said Yumi.

"The kissing club?" asked Rachel.

Everyone giggled again.

"We should print out T-shirts," said Yumi.

"That's seriously so awesome," said Claire.

"The T-shirt idea or Annabelle's boyfriend?" asked Yumi.

"Both," said Claire. "But mostly the Annabelle and Oliver news. Listen to how cute their names sound together: Annabelle and Oliver. Oliver and Annabelle. Adorable!"

"I know," I said.

"I'll bet it makes up for getting cut from the talent show," said Rachel.

Just then Claire elbowed her. "Don't bring it up."

"Sorry!" said Rachel.

"Don't feel bad," said Claire. "You're not the only one. My sister's friend Harrison made up a rap that had swear words in it, and Ms. Benson cut him off before he even finished his performance."

"I saw Mr. Beller do the same thing to the guy who burped the Pledge of Allegiance," said Yumi. "Which isn't fair because that takes talent."

"And now Taylor's trying to get some seventh-grade dance troop disqualified," Rachel told us.

"How come?" asked Claire.

"She claims they stole her choreography, but I think she's really mad because they're both dancing to Lady Gaga," Rachel explained.

"She did warn everyone against that," I said.

"Right—and everyone should listen to her because why?" asked Claire.

"Because otherwise she'll try and get them dis-qualified," said Rachel. "She's such a diva."

"Hey, what's Oliver doing for the talent show?" asked Claire.

"He's drawing portraits of people," I said. "Lightning-fast ones."

"Are you going to model for him?" asked Yumi.

"No, he's picking random people in the audience," I said. "That's part of his talent—being able to draw strangers from scratch."

"When are you seeing him next?" asked Rachel.

I glanced at my watch. "Right after lunch. Ugh!"

"Ugh?" asked Yumi.

All my friends stared at me, totally confused.

"Whoops, did I say that out loud?" I asked, feeling my face turn red.

"Yeah, what's up?" asked Rachel.

"I'm not sure how I'm supposed to act around him now that he's officially my boyfriend."

"Walk into class and give him a kiss on the lips," said Claire.

"I can't!" I cried.

"Relax," said Rachel, holding up her hands. "She's only kidding."

"Oh," I said, feeling silly. "Right, I should've known that. But what am I supposed to do? What if everything's different now? What if it's awkward? What if he tries to hold my hand under the table? Or what if *he* tries to kiss *me*?"

"He won't," said Rachel.

"But don't you *want* to kiss him?" asked Emma.

"Of course, but not at school."

"If Nathan went to school here, I'd totally kiss him in front of everyone," said Yumi.

Yumi's boyfriend, Nathan, lives in Michigan. They met each other in Hawaii over winter vacation and they haven't seen each other since. They spend a lot of time texting and talking on the phone, and they miss each other terribly. I understood what she was saying but still . . .

"If Nathan went to school here, you'd feel weird about holding hands," I said. "I'm sure you would."

"It's hard to imagine," said Yumi. "But maybe . . ."

"Definitely," said Emma. "I get what you're saying, Annabelle. When Phil and I were going out we hardly even talked at school. And sometimes we ignored each other completely, so don't worry."

"But I don't want to ignore Oliver. We always talked before we were going out. Are we supposed to talk less now that we're actually a couple? Because that sounds like a bad deal."

"You're the one who's embarrassed to be seen with him," said Rachel.

"I'm not embarrassed of him, only the situation. And I'm not even really embarrassed. It's more like I don't know how to act."

"You'll be fine," said Claire. "I'm sure you'll still get to hang out."

"But now there's all this added pressure," I said.

"Only if you create it," said Claire.

Suddenly my stomach felt twitchy. I put down my tuna fish sandwich, unable to eat another bite.

Ten minutes later I walked into science class. Oliver smiled at me and waved. I waved back, then walked over and sat next to him. Not because we were boyfriend and girlfriend. We always sat next to each other, even when we were just friends and even before that—when we were virtual strangers. And not only virtual—we were total strangers.

To think that back in September I was disappointed

about having to sit next to Oliver. If I could build a time machine and go back in time and tell myself that not only would I love Birchwood Middle School, but I'd also have a genuine real live boyfriend, well, there'd be no point in traveling back in time to tell myself that because I'd never believe myself.

"You okay?" asked Oliver.

"Yeah, why?" I asked quickly.

"You seem nervous," he said.

"Nope. I'm good."

He leaned in close and whispered, "So you're not going to break up with me?"

"No," I said quickly, and then laughed. "I still feel the same way about you now that lunch is over."

Oliver glanced at his watch. "That's cool. So we've been together for over an hour."

"And they said it wouldn't last."

Oliver's eyebrows furrowed together and his smile disappeared as he asked, "Who said that?"

"No one that I know of," I said. "I was kidding."

"Oh—sorry," said Oliver.

"No need to be," I replied. "I guess it was a bad joke."

"Hey, Spazabelle," said Tobias, coming into class as soon as the bell rang. "What's up?" He knocked my science book off the desk and it fell to the ground with a loud bang.

"Have too much sugar at lunch?" I asked, narrowing my eyes at him.

"Nope. Not enough," Tobias replied.

Meanwhile, Oliver bent down to pick up my book.

The move was so sweet and chivalrous I couldn't help but blush. "Thanks," I whispered.

"Anytime," he replied softly.

"So where's Pepper?" asked Tobias. "Knocking someone over or stealing someone's pie?"

I crossed my arms over my chest and glared. "Leave my dog out of this."

Tobias smiled mischievously and turned to Oliver. "You should've seen Annabelle yesterday. She was freaking out. And her dog was out of control—destroying everything. Annabelle was chasing him and screaming and—"

"I wasn't screaming," I said.

"Were, too," said Tobias.

"I was not," I said.

"Were, too."

"Geez, Tobias. Are you in the third grade?" asked Oliver.

"Takes one to know one," said Tobias.

I laughed. "One what? A third grader? That doesn't make any sense."

"Hey, can I borrow your pencil?" asked Tobias, grabbing it right out of my hand before I had agreed to anything.

"No, it's my only one," I said.

"Too bad," said Tobias, keeping my pencil, clearly enjoying himself way too much.

"Give it back," said Oliver. "And leave her alone!"

"Why? What do you care?" asked Tobias.

"I just do," said Oliver.

"What, are you in love with her?" he asked. When neither of us answered, Tobias launched into song, as if we were all on the kindergarten playground. "Oliver and Annabelle, sitting in a tree. K-i-s-s-i-n-g. First comes love. Then comes marriage. Then comes—ow!"

Suddenly Tobias slipped off his chair and landed on the floor.

Except he didn't merely slip off the chair. Oliver knocked him off. Then he kicked his chair over.

It clattered against the tile floor loudly. Suddenly the room went silent. Everyone stared at us, including our teacher, Ms. Roberts, who'd just walked into the room. "The late bell, in case you haven't heard it, has rung. And I'd like to begin class, unless there's a problem," she said sternly.

"Nope. Not at all," said Tobias. "I, um, slipped."

He stood quickly and righted his chair.

"Let's not slip again," Ms. Roberts said. "Deal?"

"Deal," said Tobias as he sat back down.

As soon as she turned her back, he punched Oliver in the arm. "Dude, you don't have to be so sensitive," he whispered.

"And you don't have to be such a jerk."

"I'm not a jerk," said Tobias. "Anyway, what's the big deal?"

"Just leave us alone."

"Us?" Tobias asked, looking back and forth between us with raised eyebrows.

Oliver and I both looked away. Ms. Roberts talked

about photosynthesis, and we all paid attention and took notes.

Forty minutes later, when class was dismissed and we began packing up our things, Tobias asked, "So what's the deal with you two?"

Neither of us said anything for a moment. Other kids in class, I noticed, lingered near our table, taking their time filing out and clearly listening in on the conversation.

Oliver took a deep breath and said, "The big deal is she's my girlfriend."

"What?" asked Tobias. "You've got to be kidding me."

"Nope," said Oliver.

Tobias looked at me for confirmation, and I nodded. "It's true."

Tobias narrowed his eyes at us. "Well, why didn't you say so?" he asked before hurrying out of the room.

Oliver and I looked at each other and laughed.

After we parted ways, something occurred to me. Oliver had declared us a couple, in public. He'd announced it to the entire class, practically. That was a big deal. Soon the whole school would know.

I'll be the object of gossip. And while that sounds like a bad thing, there is such a thing as the right kind of gossip. And Oliver and me, our coupledom (or is it couplehood?) is the perfect example.

This was amazing.

Stupendous.

If I were half British like Oliver, I'd say "brilliant."

My whole body buzzed and zinged with excitement. *I have a boyfriend. I have a boyfriend. I have a boyfriend.* The words raced through my mind and I could not stop smiling. It seriously felt like the best day of school, ever.

I knew I had to savor the moment. And it's a good thing I did. Because before I knew it, life got pretty complicated.

chapter eleven
romeo and juliet and the pta

What's going on with you?" asked Rachel when we walked home from school that day.

"She's in love," Yumi said before I could answer.

I shoved her playfully. "I am not in love. I am in serious like."

"No, you *love* Oliver," Yumi said.

"I'm too young to be in love," I insisted.

"Juliet was only fourteen," said Rachel.

"Who?" I asked.

"Juliet of *Romeo and Juliet*. You know—Shakespeare," said Rachel.

"Oh yeah, I've heard of him," I joked. "But things were different back then. With all the wars and disease and food shortages going on, people only lived to be, like, fifty. So being fourteen was more like being twenty-four or even thirty in today's world. A totally different reality."

My mom teaches a Shakespeare class, so I felt pretty confident with this analysis.

"Are you saying your feelings are less real because you're eleven?" asked Yumi.

"Considering that people got married in their teens, I'd have to say yes," I said. "The whole world is different and I live in the world, so my feelings are different, too. Not less real. Simply less, well, intense. And I'm eleven and three-quarters. Practically twelve, thank you very much."

"What would you do if you were forbidden from seeing Oliver?" asked Rachel. "Like what if your parents were mortal enemies?"

"I don't think that'll happen," I said. "Our moms are on the PTA together."

"But he lives in Canyon Ranch," said Rachel. "That's where all the mega-mansions are. Maybe his family won't approve of you because you're from the wrong side of the tracks."

I worried about this for half a second because it's true—Oliver's family is way richer than mine. Their house is huge and ours is normal. His mom drives a fancy, new-smelling car. My mom's Honda is almost as old as me. His family goes to Europe every year. I've never been off the North American continent. Was Rachel right?

Suddenly Rachel and Yumi burst out laughing.

"What's so funny?" I asked.

"I was only teasing," said Rachel. "But you should've seen your face. You're, like, totally worried."

"Because you love him!" Yumi said in a singsongy voice.

"Who knew getting my first boyfriend would turn my friends into freaks?" I asked.

"When are you seeing lover boy again?" asked Rachel.

"I don't know, and please don't call him that!"

"Maybe you should go to a movie this weekend," said Rachel. "And Yumi and I can go, too, and spy on you."

"I'm sure you can find something better to do with your time," I said to them.

By now we were at the corner of Oak and Pacific. Yumi waved good-bye, and Rachel and I continued to our street in silence.

When I walked into my house I noticed something weird. My mom and Ted were both home. I checked my watch. It was only four o'clock. Usually both of them get home after five. I was going to ask them what was up, but as soon as they realized I was home they stopped talking abruptly, like they had something to hide.

The two of them sat at the kitchen table with serious expressions on their faces. Also? My mom looked tired and stressed. She had heavy black circles under her puffy eyes, as if she hadn't slept all night.

Obviously they didn't want me to hear what they were saying. Were they fighting? And did it have anything to do with Patricia? What did she want with Ted?

I wanted to ask, but a large part of me didn't want to know.

Also, maybe I was looking for something to be

wrong. If I hadn't picked up the phone, if I hadn't seen Ted and Patricia having cake last week, would I even be thinking these thoughts? Was my mother really upset, or was it all in my head?

"What's up?" I asked.

"Nothing," my mom and Ted said at the same time.

I didn't believe them, but I didn't feel like saying so at the moment. "What's for dinner?" I asked instead.

"Dinner." My mom frowned. "I just ate, actually. Sorry, honey. I'm not feeling great. I have a headache. I think I need to lie down."

I checked my watch again. It was still only four. Who ate dinner before four? Was it even possible to eat dinner before four? Wouldn't that actually be called lunch or a very large snack?

I would've asked, but my mom had already left the room.

I looked at Ted, who smiled at me guiltily. Like he was hiding something.

"I'll fix you something," he said, standing up. "How about pasta?"

I still felt suspicious around Ted, but the thing is, he's a great cook and I was hungry.

"Okay."

"Do you want spaghetti sauce or butter and herbs?"

I sighed before I answered, as if it were a huge chore deciding. "Butter and herbs. And how come my mom is acting so weird?"

Whoops. So much for acting normal!

"How is she acting weird?" he asked me, as if he had no idea what I was referring to, but I knew that was impossible.

"Forgetful, tired, hungry," I said.

As I suspected, he didn't deny it. "You should ask your mother," was all he'd say. His voice sounded mysterious, like he had a secret. But what could it be?

Something in the back of my brain began to whirr. Something didn't make sense. I didn't know what was going on, but I couldn't come out and ask. Problem was, I wasn't sure I wanted to find out.

chapter twelve
paper, scissors, rock stars

Usually Rachel picks me up before school. I don't like to go to her house because her older brother, Jackson, is kind of annoying. He loves teasing me and will pull my ponytail, call me Spaz, and ask me if I looked in the mirror before I stepped outside, or if I bought my clothes at the ninety-nine-cent store. Meanwhile, they don't even sell clothes at the ninety-nine-cent store—I know because I've been. But that's not the kind of thing I want to get into at 7:30 in the morning.

And today I couldn't wait to get out of my house. My mom was cleaning out the den, and not only that—she was cleaning the den cheerfully. My mom hates to clean, and the fact that she seemed excited about it . . . well, it made me nervous. She should've been getting ready for work, except she told me she wasn't going today because she had a doctor's appointment later on.

"Are you okay?" I asked.

"I'm fine," she replied. "It's just a checkup."

So I went over to Rachel's house early. Luckily, Jackson didn't even seem to be home. Rachel answered the door, and she had a fresh-looking Band-Aid on her forehead.

"What happened?" I asked.

"Just another unicycle-related injury," she said, raising her fingertips to her head.

I cringed. "You do wear a helmet, right?"

"Well, now I do," she replied. "Don't worry. It's all going to be worth it. Those judges are going to be blown away."

"Hey, speaking of judges. I forgot to tell you—I'm one of them."

"What?" asked Rachel. "No way!"

"Way! Mr. Beller asked me last week."

Rachel shoved me playfully, but hard enough to make me stumble. "You've known for days and you're only telling me now?"

"Sorry. I guess I forgot."

"You forgot? I think you have an acute case of Oliver-on-the-brain. Wait until Yumi finds out."

As soon as we got to the corner Rachel blurted out my big news. "Annabelle is one of the judges for the talent show."

"Awesome with cheese and bacon bits!" said Yumi, giving me a high five.

"I know—it'll be fun," I said. "I'm glad I'll still be a part of it, anyway."

"More important than that—you can make sure one of us wins," said Rachel.

"And that the other one comes in second place," Yumi added.

"Huh?" I asked.

"Oh, come on. You know your friends are the most talented kids in school," said Rachel. "But how are you going to pick? I suppose it's only fair to let Emma and Claire in on this, too. Maybe we should draw straws."

"Do people really do that?" I asked.

"I don't know. I've never seen it," Rachel said with a shrug. "We could flip a coin instead."

"Or we could do rock-paper-scissors," said Yumi.

"You guys are kidding, right?" I asked.

Except apparently they weren't because they went ahead and counted to three, and Rachel made a rock and Yumi made paper.

"I win!" Yumi cheered.

"We're doing best out of three," said Rachel.

"Too late. You need to call that before we start," said Yumi.

"This is just practice," said Rachel. "We have to give Claire and Emma a chance, too."

"Don't you think it'll be highly suspicious if I vote for my best friends?" I asked.

"Not at all. Everyone expects it," said Rachel.

"She's right. It's like running for school president. You don't nominate the kid you think will do the best job. You nominate your friends," said Yumi.

"I do?" I asked.

"Yes," said Yumi and Rachel at the same time.

"I can't believe you didn't know that," Rachel said. "And I'm insanely jealous that you get to be the boss. That's so much better than performing!"

"There are other judges," I reminded her.

"I know, but you're one of six. One of three student judges and the only sixth-grade student judge. You are so lucky!" Rachel said.

I couldn't deny what she was saying. I was lucky. I was the sixth-grade judge. I had a boyfriend, and not just that: I had the sweetest and most wonderful boyfriend in the world. Life was pretty perfect. Of course, there was one factor I forgot about. And that factor's name is Tobias.

As soon as I walked into science that afternoon the trouble began. Tobias said to me, "Why are you so dressed up, Annabelle?"

"What do you mean?" I asked innocently. Okay, I had maybe spent a little more time than usual on my hair, and I was wearing my favorite jeans and I'd borrowed one of Claire's new tops. I felt spiffy, although I'd never say so. *Spiffy* is kind of a nerdy term even though it's a good and accurate one, too.

Maybe I decided to spend more time on my appearance because of the whole boyfriend situation. But it's not like I decided to wear a prom dress. Or any dress, for that matter. And it's not like I was about to admit that to Tobias, but it turns out I didn't have to. He kind of guessed it. And when I say "kind of," what I really mean is "completely." The dude nailed it.

"Did you dress up for your BOYFRIEND?" asked Tobias, with a heavy emphasis on the word *boyfriend*. His voice carried so loudly everyone in the entire room heard. Except he said it like having a boyfriend was something I should be ashamed of, and that doesn't make any sense because there's nothing shameful about me and Oliver.

I rolled my eyes and told Tobias to give it a rest. Then I sat down and buried my head in my book.

When Oliver showed up, he said hi, and before I could say hi in response, Tobias said, "Hi, LOVER BOY," in a singsongy and super-annoying tone of voice.

Oliver punched him in the arm. And while it was good that he'd defended me and himself and us as a couple, it wasn't cool how he avoided looking at me all through class. Like he was ashamed of me!

Once when I looked over at Oliver, Tobias began making smooching noises and pretended to make out with the back of his hand.

It was hard not to feel self-conscious and weird.

Embarrassed, too.

No, make that humiliated.

As soon as class got out, Oliver gave me a quick wave and then bolted like the room was on fire or they were giving away free marshmallows to the first ten kids out the door.

Is that what having a boyfriend is going to be like?

A small part of me feared that Tobias was going to ruin our entire relationship. Meanwhile, we've been together for less than a week. We've hardly even had a relationship.

chapter thirteen
judgment day

After school the next day I found Taylor and Nikki waiting for me at my locker. Both of them had huge smiles plastered on their faces. I guess they'd made up. I wondered if their dance routine was still going to happen. It's not like I could ask. Not them, anyway. Although I'm sure Rachel knew the answer . . . possibly before Taylor and her friends.

"Hey, Annabelle!" they both yelled, their voices high-pitched and super-enthusiastic.

"Hi," I replied cautiously. The thing is, I don't totally trust Taylor and Nikki.

Actually, I don't trust them at all.

Taylor's favorite hobby is making other girls squirm. And she's good at it, too.

She's pretty on the outside—with shiny dark hair, green eyes, and perfect clothes—and kind of catty on the inside. And when I say "kind of" I actually mean *very*.

Nikki isn't as bad one-on-one, but something about being with Taylor makes her vicious.

I'd never go out of my way to be cruel to Taylor

and Nikki—I know that's a big fat waste of time. But I'm not going to go out of my way to be nice to them, either.

Except that's exactly what they were doing to me. I didn't know why they were acting that way, but I did know to proceed with caution. Middle school is like a minefield. One misstep and *bam!* Your whole world can explode.

"Hey, guys," I said, since I couldn't exactly ignore them: (a) that's not my style, and (b) they were blocking my locker.

"Annabelle, you're just the girl I wanted to see," Taylor said, putting her arm around my shoulder. She smelled like fancy shampoo or maybe it was perfume or maybe—probably—it was both.

"Oh my gosh, I love those shoes!" Nikki said, pointing down at my yellow high-tops.

Yellow high-tops that just a few months ago she called clown shoes. Something I couldn't help but remind her of as I shrugged out of Taylor's grasp. "You like them?" I asked. "I got them at the circus."

"The circus?" Nikki blinked at me without a clue. Could she have not remembered how she'd insulted me? Or was she pretending not to remember? She flipped her hair over her shoulder and said, "I haven't been there. Is that some new store at the mall?"

I couldn't tell if she was kidding or not. Somehow she didn't seem to be. I didn't bother to clarify, though, because I was too curious about her odd behavior. And Taylor's, too. "What's up?" I asked.

"Nothing," said Taylor. "We just wanted to say hi. Catch up. We should hang out sometime."

Suddenly Rachel and Yumi approached. Taylor backed off as if she were a vampire and my friends wore necklaces made of garlic.

Or like Taylor was her regular self and my friends wore necklaces from last season!

"What was that about?" asked Rachel, once Taylor and Nikki were gone.

"No idea," I said.

"Are you ready to go home?" asked Yumi.

"I can't. I have my first official meeting with the talent show judges."

"Cool! Call me later and tell me all about it," said Rachel.

"And me, too," said Yumi.

"Will do," I promised them before heading to the gym.

By the time I arrived, most of the judges were already there. Someone had arranged six folding chairs into a circle. I took the one next to the seventh-grade judge—a boy named Hugo Ross.

Hugo wears large, chunky glasses with tortoiseshell frames. He has one blue eye and one green eye. He's cute and quiet, which makes him seem mysterious. Oh, and he's also the photographer for the yearbook, so he often wears a clunky old camera around his neck.

And now that I was close to him, I realized I had the same exact camera.

"Hey, I have one of those," I said, pointing.

"Really?" he asked.

I nodded. "My stepdad got a new one, so he gave me his. I have some cool lenses, too. A wide-angle one and a fish-eye."

"You're lucky. I'm saving up for the fish eye," said Hugo.

"Oh, you should borrow mine sometime," I said.

"That would be awesome. Thanks."

"Sure. It's no biggie."

"It is," said Hugo. "So who are your favorite photographers?"

"Huh?" I asked.

"I like Ansel Adams. You know—he did those great nature shots of Yosemite—everything is black and white and so dramatic and severe."

"Riiight," I replied slowly, stretching out the word. I don't know why I said that because, honestly, I didn't know any photographers. I decided to come clean. "I haven't heard of him. I actually just started taking pictures. It's all pretty new to me."

Rather than laugh at me or look at me like I was some super-dork, Hugo said, "I have an Ansel Adams wall calendar. I'll bring it in tomorrow and show you some of his work."

Just then Mr. Beller called the meeting to order. "I assume everyone knows each other, but just in case, we'll go around and introduce ourselves," he said. "I'm Mr. Beller and I teach sixth-grade English."

"I'm Annabelle," I said. "And I'm the sixth-grade judge."

"Hugo, seventh-grade representative," said Hugo, giving a salute to the rest of us.

After Ms. Lerner and Ms. Benson gave us their names, I raised my hand. "Isn't there supposed to be an eighth-grade judge, too?" I asked.

"Wait, don't start without me," Rachel's brother, Jackson, yelled as he jogged into the seat next to me. "Sorry I'm late," he said to the teachers. "I had to talk my way out of detention."

"I'm sure you did," said Mr. Beller.

"We're happy you can join us," Ms. Benson added. "I think you'll have fun with this."

"Judging my fellow students?" Jackson asked, rubbing his hands together and grinning a sly grin. "It's gonna be amazing."

"And it's wonderful that you're all mature enough to handle the responsibility," said Ms. Lerner. "You should be honored that you've been chosen—all three of you—and act accordingly."

I stifled a laugh. Jackson didn't. He laughed out loud, but he also managed to sit up straighter and pay attention.

"Now that we're all here we can go over the rules and the format," said Ms. Benson. "We have thirty acts in the show. If everyone has five minutes, that means there will be one hundred and eighty minutes of performing. Who can tell me how many hours that is?"

When no one answered he called on me. "Annabelle?"

"Three hours," I answered after doing some quick math in my head. "But I didn't realize there'd be a pop quiz."

The rest of the judges laughed.

"Three hours—plus, we'll need time to clear people off the stage," said Ms. Lerner. "And there's an intermission when we'll sell beverages and snacks. That'll take twenty minutes, which means . . ."

"Which means we're looking at a very long night," said Mr. Beller.

"And a fun night," I said. "Birchwood Middle School's got so much talent! Simon Cowell should come visit."

"Oh, he's my role model," said Jackson with a snicker. He and Hugo gave each other a high five.

"I'm glad you brought up the judging process, Jackson," said Mr. Beller. "This should go without saying, but we're trusting you all to leave your personal feelings at the door. This is about talent. This is not about voting for your best friend or your boyfriend or your girlfriend. You have all been chosen because we trust you."

"Now let's talk about the specifics," Ms. Lerner said. "The six of us will sit in the front row, and it's important that you pay close attention for the entire show. There are three categories we're interested in: skill, originality, and overall entertainment value. Each category will get a number on a scale of zero to five. Add those up and you get your number—something between zero and fifteen. Then we'll combine all six scores to get something between zero and ninety. The act with the most points wins the competition."

"What if there's a tie?" I asked.

"If there's a tie, we'll have more than one winner," said Ms. Benson.

"What's the prize?" asked Jackson.

"The prize is the glory and pride that goes along with being declared the winner of the talent show," Ms. Lerner explained.

"No, really. What is it?" asked Jackson.

No one answered him, and Mr. Beller decided to end our meeting early.

chapter fourteen
miss popular

A few days later, I ran into Fred the baker. I'd been avoiding him since the Pepper pie-eating incident, and if I'd seen him coming I would've taken off in the other direction. Now I was filled with dread. Except rather than yell at me, he handed me a small silver gift bag with a silky red ribbon tied into a bow.

"What's this?" I asked, looking at the bag nervously.

"Homemade dog treats," he said. "For Pepper."

Was this guy joking? I opened the bag and pulled out a bone-shaped cookie. It smelled like peanut butter. "Is it poisoned?" I wondered aloud, only half-kidding.

Fred looked shocked. The kid actually turned pale—which was quite a feat because he was already pretty pasty. "No, of course not. I would never do that."

"I'm joking," I said. "You know, because my dog messed up your act."

"I know, but I still qualified for the talent show," said Fred. "So what happened at the audition doesn't even matter. And this is so you know there's no hard feelings."

"Okay," I said, staring at the biscuits. "Thank you."

"They're fine for people to eat, too. Really, they're just made out of peanut butter, flour, and oil. My mom breeds Goldendoodles, and she has an entire cookbook for dogs. That's where this recipe is from."

"You really made these for my dog?" I asked.

"Yup," Fred said with a nod.

I opened up my locker and placed the dog-biscuit bag inside. "That's sweet."

"Hopefully Pepper will think so, too."

Fred took off before I had a chance to ask him why he was being so nice to my dog.

As I headed to homeroom, a popular seventh grader named Heather Willamette waved hello. Figuring her friend must be behind me, I ignored her. But then she called after me.

"You're Annabelle Stevens, right?" she asked.

I turned around. "Yup. That's me."

"Hi, I'm Heather." She stuck out her hand.

"Hi," I said, shaking. "Did you want something?"

"Yes, I want to meet you," said Heather.

Her comment seemed like the elaborate setup to a cruel practical joke. Except it wasn't. And somehow my day only got weirder. The sneeziest member of the string quartet—the guy Pepper had tortured at the audition—offered to let me cut in front of him in the lunch line.

Another one said she liked my hair band. Yes, my

hair band. Let me describe my hair band to you: it's thin and beige and it blends into my hair.

I pointed this plainness out to her and she sort of stumbled and said, "I know. That's why I like it."

Huh? I really didn't know how to respond to her, so I smiled and said, "Thanks."

Then, after I got my pizza, it was hard to make my way back to my regular table because everyone wanted to talk to me.

"Hi, Annabelle."

"How's it going, Annabelle?"

"Yo, Annabelle!"

"Hey there, Anna."

"Does anyone ever call you Bella?"

"ANNABELLA!" (*Screamed from the other end of the hallway with an Italian accent.*)

"Annabelle, I love your hair."

"Annabelle, you are so funny."

"Where'd you get that jacket, Annabelle? It's super-cute."

"Annabelle, everyone tells me you're so cool. How come we've never hung out?"

"Arrabelle, wait, what's that? Your name is Annabelle? Right—I knew that . . . I totally did. Please don't hold it against me."

By the time lunch ended my cheeks hurt from smiling so much.

It's like suddenly I was the most popular girl in school, but that didn't make any sense. Popular girls at Birchwood Middle School are usually more outgoing.

Not to put myself down or anything. I'm friendly enough but kind of shy.

Nice but not bubbly. In other words, my personality doesn't overflow like a shaken-up can of orange soda. Or any kind of soda, not even plain seltzer.

I love my friends, but we are not the coolest of the cool. We're simply regular, middle of the road—kind of cool and kind of not—which is fine by me.

Oliver Banks, however, is extremely popular.

It's probably his cuteness and sweetness combined with his half British–half Jamaican-ness and also his awesomeness at sports. Oliver has lots of *nesses*.

I wondered if all this new attention had anything to do with Oliver. Word must've gotten out that we were a couple. And people must've suddenly realized that if he liked me enough to be my boyfriend, then maybe there was something more to me.

That's what I thought until I ran into Hugo after school.

He had his calendar for me.

"Thanks," I said. "I'll bring you the fish-eye lens tomorrow. Sorry I forgot it."

"No worries," said Hugo. "I'd love to borrow it, but that's not the only reason I'm lending you my calendar."

"Oh, I know," I said.

"I feel like I'm the only person in school without an ulterior motive," said Hugo.

"What do you mean?" I asked.

He smiled. "Haven't you noticed kids being extra nice to you as of late?"

"Yeah," I said. "I just figured it was because, well . . ." I didn't want to share my theory because it seemed too embarrassing. But wait a second. "Are you saying kids have been nice to you, too?"

"Of course," said Hugo. "We're in the same boat, right?"

Did Hugo have a more popular girlfriend or boyfriend I didn't know about? Or, wait a second . . . As the truth slowly dawned on me, I turned red. "You mean people are kissing up to us because we're judges?" I asked.

"Yes, of course. Why else?" Hugo asked, grinning at me.

"No reason!" I said quickly. "I've got to go."

I took off, fast, before I could embarrass myself further.

When I got home, the house was empty except for Pepper. We curled up on my bed and I rubbed his tummy, thinking about school and friends and all the weirdness. It was nice being super-popular, but knowing it wasn't genuine made me feel weird.

"I can't let all these people get to me," I told Pepper. "I have to stay tough, vote for the best act, don't you think?"

Pepper raised his head and looked me in the eye. Obviously he couldn't understand what I was saying. Yet something told me if he could, he'd agree.

chapter fifteen
surprise! no, make that a double

Later that week, I heard a horrible retching noise coming from my mom's bathroom. I peeked inside and saw her on her knees, hanging over the toilet bowl. "Are you okay?" I asked.

"Fine," she said. "Could you please get me a glass of water?"

"Sure," I said. "But do you need anything else? You seem pretty sick. Maybe I should call your doctor."

"No, don't. I'm fine," my mom said. "All I need is some water."

I ran downstairs and got her water with ice.

"Are you sure you're okay?" I asked, when I found her again, sitting on her bed, propped up against some fluffy pillows.

"I'm fine, Annabelle. But we need to talk."

Those words were hardly ever followed by positive news. I sat down on my mom's bed, crossed my legs, and rested my chin on my fists. "What is it? Are you sick? Is it bad?"

In the back of my mind I figured that maybe she

was so sick with worry about Ted and Patricia's relationship (assuming that she knew) that she'd made herself physically ill.

I once saw this show about how some ailments can be caused or at least exacerbated by psychological stress. Some doctors believe that even serious diseases can be treated with a healthy attitude and a positive outlook on life. Of course, other doctors think all of that's crazy. But I was willing to be open-minded.

"Nothing's wrong, sweetie. I have good news. I'm pregnant!"

"What?" I yelled.

"We're having a baby."

"No way!" Fear. Excitement. Shock. And a gazillion other emotions I couldn't even identify pulsed through my body so that all I could think to do was scream.

My mom screamed, too, laughing.

I bounced up and down on the bed. My mom bounced up and down on the bed. Then we hugged. "This is amazing!" I said.

She cracked up and I started laughing and soon we were both crying.

"How did this happen?" I asked.

My mom burst out laughing again.

I felt my cheeks heat up and I giggled. "Never mind."

"Phew—I'm glad we don't have to have *that* conversation again," my mom said.

"Yeah, I know enough—I don't need details," I said.

"But if you want to—we can. You must always come to me with any questions."

I covered my ears with my hands. "Let's not get into this now. I meant, when did this happen? No, I don't need to know that, either. I just don't know what to say first. This is crazy news. I didn't even know you and Ted wanted a baby. You did plan this, right?" I asked.

"Yes, of course," my mom said.

"Wow!" I said. "I'm speechless. I mean, other than telling you I'm shocked speechless, I don't know what to say."

"How about I tell you when I'm due?" said my mom.

"Okay, when are you due?"

"October thirty-first."

"That's awesome," I said. "Wait a minute. That's Halloween."

"I know!" my mom said.

"The baby can't come on Halloween," I said, frowning. "It's my favorite holiday."

My mom stared at me, tilting her head, her smile fading ever so slightly. "Well, the baby may come before or after, but I'm certainly not going to stop him or her from arriving on Halloween."

Him or her—that sounded so strange. "So you don't know if you're having a boy or a girl?" I asked.

"Not yet. It's too early to tell. We can find out next month if we want to, but we haven't decided yet if we want to know."

"This is crazy," I said. "We have to find out!"

"Well, I'll take your opinion into consideration, but there are other people involved."

I hardly heard what she said. "I can't believe I'm going to have a brother or sister."

"You already have a stepbrother," my mom reminded me.

"Oh, yeah," I said. "But Jason doesn't really count."

"He doesn't?" asked my mom. "Don't tell him that."

"You know what I mean," I said. "He's old and he doesn't live here."

"I know—I get it," said my mom.

"A baby is a whole different story," I said.

"I agree."

Thinking about Jason made me think about Patricia. I'd been debating whether or not to tell my mom what I saw in the kitchen the other day, and now I realized I had no choice.

I took a deep breath and tried to figure out how to break it to her gently.

"What's wrong, Annabelle?" she asked. "You don't seem so excited."

"I am," I said. "But I need to tell you something about Ted. I saw him last week in the kitchen, and he was eating cake with . . . with Patricia. You know—Jason's mom. His ex-wife. And she called last week, too. I don't know why, but . . ."

My mom sucked in her lips. I thought she was going to cry, but instead she burst out laughing.

"What's so funny?" I asked.

"No, I'm sorry. It's just—I know that Patricia and Ted have been spending time together."

"You do?" I asked.

"Yes, because Patricia is a real estate broker," my mom explained.

"Ted's moving?" I asked, more confused than ever.

"Not only Ted," my mom said, holding out her hands. "Surprise! We all are."

chapter sixteen
one tough chick

We can't move!" I yelled. "We just got here, practically, and I'm not going to become one of those girls who's always the new kid. Do you know how hard it was starting over back in September? Or how long it took me to fit in? Or to finally understand how things work here? And I love it here. There's no way you can make me leave."

"Wait a second. Annabelle, sweetie—please relax. We're not moving out of Westlake. We're looking for a bigger house in this neighborhood."

"Oh," I said. "Well, that changes things. But are you sure?"

"I am absolutely positive. We are not going to uproot you again. Not when you've adjusted so well. We're thrilled for you. Your friends, and Pepper, your new boyfriend—"

"Mom!" I yelled.

"What?" she asked, grinning at me. "Do you think I didn't notice that you have a boyfriend? I know I've been a little spacey as of late, but I'm not completely clueless."

"Okay, okay," I said. "But please don't talk about my boyfriend. It's weird."

"My lips are sealed," she said. "But just so you know, Ted and I love Oliver. He's a very sweet boy, and we couldn't be more excited for you."

I felt squirmy with embarrassment, but also happy that my mom liked my boyfriend. Oh, and embarrassed to be happy about that. It shouldn't matter what my mom thinks. I'm old enough to make my own decisions, right? Romeo and Juliet didn't care what their parents thought. Of course, they ended up dead, so they're probably not the best example.

"And if you have any questions—anything you want to talk about . . ."

"Mom!" I yelled.

"I'm only saying—"

"Okay, fine. I'll let you know. But more important—I can't believe we're having a baby," I said.

"I know. I can't believe it, either."

"What are we going to name it?"

"You mean him or her," my mom said.

"Him or her. Whatever you say. Do you want a boy or a girl?" I asked.

"Either way—as long as he or she is as wonderful as you."

"That's sweet," I said.

"Sweet and true," my mom replied. She kissed me on the forehead and then suggested that I get started on my homework. As if I could concentrate!

At dinner that night, the three of us talked about

the new house. And Pepper danced around our feet with his tail wagging, hoping for table scraps.

"We're looking at some places in Canyon Ranch," Ted told me.

"That's where Oliver and Emma live," I said.

"Good, so you'll have friends there," my mom said. "It's not that big of an area. I'm sure you'll be able to walk to their places."

"It'll be weird not to be across the street from Rachel," I said.

"I know, honey," said my mom.

"We won't get to walk to school together anymore."

"Maybe you'll get to walk with Emma and Oliver," said Ted.

What if I moved next door to Oliver? How great would that be? But what if Oliver thought I convinced my family to move just so I could be closer to him? Like our whole family was stalking his whole family. I hope he realized this is simply a lucky coincidence. And I hoped we would still be together by the time the move happened.

"When are we going?" I asked.

"I'm not sure, exactly," said my mom. "We haven't found a house yet, and even if we did tomorrow, it would take a few months."

"So will we be moving before or after the baby comes?" I asked.

"Again, I don't know. But as soon as we figure it out, you'll be the first to know," said my mom.

After dinner I called Rachel to tell her the big

news, but she wasn't home. Neither was Yumi. Oliver's mom told me he was at his painting class, but I did manage to talk to Claire and Emma.

Emma said she was jealous. As an only child, she wished she could get a baby brother or sister, but her parents are probably too old.

Claire was ecstatic. She said I'd make an awesome big sister, and as the youngest in her family, she'd definitely give me pointers.

I didn't get to tell Rachel and Yumi the news until our walk to school the next day. But as soon as the three of us were together, I blurted it out. "Guess what? My mom and Ted are having a baby!"

"That's awesome!" said Yumi. "You'll love being a big sister. I love it. My baby sister, Olive, is so cute. And because my parents were so afraid I'd be jealous of all the attention she got when she was born, they got me tons of cool presents."

"Really?" I asked. "I didn't realize I'd get new stuff."

Yumi nodded. "Totally. You'll clean up. Start making a list. It'll be bigger than Christmas."

"Cool!"

"I wonder if that's why Jackson is so mean to me," said Rachel. "Because my parents never gave him presents when I was born."

"Hey, you're not going to have to share a room, are you?" asked Yumi.

"I don't think so," I said. "My mom says we're moving."

Rachel stopped in her tracks and yelled, "What?"

"Don't worry," I said. "We're staying in the neigh-borhood. They're just looking for a larger place. My mom promised I'd get to stay at Birchwood."

"That's a relief. But I can't believe you won't live across the street."

"That part will stink," I said. "But it's a while away."

"I hope so," said Rachel. "I wonder who'll move in next."

"Maybe a cute boy," said Yumi. "How cool would that be?"

"Very," said Rachel.

"Hey, I'm not even gone yet," I said.

"So what's the latest with Oliver?" asked Yumi.

"Things are good, but Tobias keeps bugging us in science and that's pretty—"

"She means, has he kissed you yet?" asked Rachel.

"No, but we've held hands."

"Again?" asked Yumi.

"No, from before, when we went out for pancakes," I reminded them.

"Yeah, we know about that," said Yumi.

"And he's coming over after school on Friday."

"Really?" asked Rachel. "That's great."

"What are you guys going to do?" asked Yumi.

"I don't know. Homework."

"You can't do homework on a Friday night. Not on your second date. That's too boring," Rachel informed me.

"Oh," I said, not realizing. "Then maybe we'll play basketball, instead."

"You guys do that all the time," said Rachel.

"Because we like playing," I reminded her.

"You need to come up with something better," said Rachel.

"Like what?" I asked.

"You'll figure it out," said Rachel. "And whatever it is—it's something that should lead to kissing."

I hoped she was right. And also not. As much as I wanted Oliver to kiss me, I worried about it, too. Holding hands was easy. I was a very good hand holder.

"Annabelle, is that you?" I heard someone yell. It was Didi, the girl who'd called me Arrabelle last week.

"Hey, Didi," I said.

As she ran to catch up to us, her long dark braids bounced against her shoulders. "Hey, how's it going? Do you walk this way every day?"

"I do," I said.

"I can't believe I've never seen you before. I usually get a ride with my big brother, but he's sick today. He drops me off before he goes to school. He's in high school. We can give you a ride sometime," she said.

This was weird. I didn't know Didi so well, and I'd never even seen her brother before. I don't think my mom would be excited about me accepting rides from strangers.

Of course, it also seemed kind of rude for her to invite me in front of Rachel and Yumi without offering them rides, too. "We walk to school together every day," I said, gesturing toward my friends, although I don't know why I had to point them out. It's not like they're invisible.

Even though Didi treated them as if they were.

She stared at me blankly, like she couldn't comprehend why I wouldn't jump at the chance to ride with her and her brother.

"It's kind of our thing," I went on.

"Okay," said Didi. "Let me know if you change your mind."

"I will," I said.

"Did I mention that my brother has a convertible? It's super-fun in the warm weather. It kind of messes up your hair, but if you wear a hat it's cool."

"I'll keep that in mind," I said.

"And you don't have to bring your own hat, either. My brother keeps extra ones in his glove compartment," she said.

"Good to know," I said.

"Or I'll get you a new one if you want," Didi said before hurrying past us.

"That was weird," said Yumi, once she was out of earshot.

"Oh, that was nothing," I told her. It was true, too. It was almost embarrassing how nice people were being to me.

When I got to science I emptied out the contents of my backpack onto the table. Out poured five sparkly pens, an eraser shaped like a pig, a key chain with a miniature cupcake attached to it, a real cupcake with a smiley face painted on it, and one small box of salt-water taffy.

"You're cleaning up!" said Tobias. "That's so not fair."

"I told everyone that whatever they gave me would not influence my decision," I said. "But people insisted anyway."

Tobias picked up a piece of saltwater taffy, unwrapped it, and popped it into his mouth.

"Hey," I said. "That's mine."

Tobias shrugged. "What's the big deal? You've got a bunch more."

When Oliver walked into the room, he said, "There's your boyfriend. If you guys need to make out, please let me know first so I can close my eyes."

"Cut it out," I said kicking him under the table.

"What? I said please."

I kicked him again but he wouldn't let up.

"I'm serious. It's the least I could do. Hi, lover boy. Did you bring Annabelle flowers? Because she was just telling me she hoped you would."

"I did not," I said through clenched teeth.

Oliver looked away, embarrassed and angry. But was he upset with me? I didn't do anything wrong. This was all about Tobias. I wished I could talk about it with Oliver, but I couldn't bring it up in class. Meanwhile, Oliver wouldn't even meet my gaze.

When Tobias began humming "Here Comes the Bride," I lost it.

"We're going out, Tobias!" I yelled. "Deal with it!"

"You are one tough chick!" Tobias replied with a laugh.

"And don't call me a chick!" I screamed right as Ms. Robinson walked through the door.

"Is there a problem here, Annabelle?" she asked.

"I don't know," I said, crossing my arms over my chest. "Ask Tobias."

chapter seventeen
don't say it!

When I got to my locker after school that day I was surprised to find Oliver waiting for me.

"Hi," I said.

"Hey, nice work in science," he said. "I'd call you one tough chick, but I know how you feel about being called a chick."

I groaned and rolled my eyes. "Hasn't it been driving you crazy, how Tobias keeps teasing us? The dude is seriously annoying."

"Yeah, but it's only because he feels left out. Since the two of us are together, that makes him the third wheel."

"So he's trying to compensate by being the squeaky wheel, too?" I asked.

"Exactly," said Oliver. "Isn't it funny how many metaphors incorporate wheels? Squeaky wheel, third wheel, spare tire."

"Who's got a spare tire?" asked Rachel, sneaking up behind us.

"Me," said Oliver, lifting up his shirt, puffing out his stomach, and pinching an inch of his flesh.

I burst out laughing and Oliver did, too.

"Fine, don't tell me!" Rachel huffed, shoving me playfully on the arm. "You and your inside jokes. It's too cute."

"Hey, you guys ready?" asked Yumi. She looked at Oliver. "Are you coming, too?"

"Yup." He hitched his backpack up farther on his shoulder. "Annabelle and I have plans."

"Cool," said Yumi.

The four of us walked home. Rachel and Yumi were in front of us. Oliver and I trailed behind. We didn't hold hands but our shoulders were close, and every once in a while we brushed up against each other.

"I pretty much have the unicycle riding and my juggling routine down," said Rachel. "But combining the unicycle riding with the juggling continues to be my downfall, literally."

"Don't injure yourself too badly before the competition," said Yumi. "Do you have to do them at the same time? Because on its own each feat is impressive. What if you did a circus act and added one more trick. Like, I don't know—do you know any magic? Or can you walk on your hands?"

"Tobias is doing magic," I said. "And his act is good, too. I saw his audition."

"Good thing you don't like him, or I'd be worried about the competition," said Rachel.

"Except I can't play favorites," I said. "I'm judging the performance, not the performer. That's what Ms. Lerner says, anyway. And I must agree."

I didn't tell my friends about how all of the special favors—all the extra gum and candy and presents and cuts in line—made me uneasy. Sure, being Miss Popularity was fun, but knowing kids were only being nice to me because I was a judge made all the attention kind of fake.

"How's the pitching coming, Yumi?" I asked.

"Are we allowed to talk about it with you?" she replied. "I don't want you to get in trouble for being biased or anything."

"Being a judge is tough," I said.

"Good thing you're tough," said Oliver.

I smiled. I guess I was getting that reputation, and I guess there are worse things to be called.

"See you guys later," said Rachel, once we got to the corner.

"Oh, you're going to Yumi's?" I asked, feeling slightly jealous even though I got to hang out with my boyfriend.

"Yup. We're baking cookies," said Rachel.

"Chocolate chip," Yumi added. "We'll try and save you some."

Once Oliver and I were alone, he grabbed my hand and he held it all the way to my house.

"What do you want to do?" I asked.

"I don't know," said Oliver.

"How about our science homework?" As soon as the question escaped from my lips, I wanted to take it back. Suggesting that we do homework together was extremely nerdy. It was Friday afternoon.

Oliver, however, surprised me. "Yeah, let's get it out of the way."

"Okay, then."

"Okay."

I let myself into the house with my key. My mom was already home. She was sitting on a lounge chair outside, sunglasses on her head, grading papers.

"Can I get you two a snack?" she asked when I popped outside to say hi.

"That's okay," I said.

"There are carrot and apple slices in the fridge. Cheese cubes, too," she said.

"Mom, you've outdone yourself," I joked.

"I try," my mom said with a sigh.

I went inside and we had the snacks. Then we pulled out our books and did our homework.

I liked the way Oliver looked when he concentrated. Sometimes he chewed on the end of his pencil. Sometimes he moved his mouth like he was swishing around water. Sometimes he bit his bottom lip.

I wondered if I was staring too hard. Maybe I shouldn't be noticing all of those things. Was that weird? Obsessive? Or was I supposed to notice things like that?

It's hard to know how to be. We always hung out, but now there was an extra layer of pressure. He wasn't just Oliver and I wasn't just Annabelle. We were Oliver and Annabelle. A couple.

Also? I knew Oliver had had other girlfriends in the past. He went out with Jesse a couple of months ago. Their relationship didn't last very long, yet I couldn't help but wonder if they did their homework together, too. Or more important, if they'd ever kissed.

I could picture it and I didn't want to picture it. I wanted to ask him but I couldn't ask him. I didn't want to know and I was dying to know.

I liked to think not, but I wasn't going to ask him. That seemed crazy jealous, and I don't want to act like a jealous girlfriend. (Even if I was, a little.)

Once we finished, Oliver said, "Want to shoot some hoops?"

"Great idea," I said.

We went out through the garage so we could grab my basketball.

The thing about Oliver is that he's not a great basketball player. At least he's not better than I am. It was almost too easy to steal the ball from him, since he didn't crouch down low when he dribbled. He let the ball bounce high, almost out of control, giving me the perfect opportunity to go in and grab it.

When the score was eight to three in my favor, he said he'd had enough. "I don't mean to be a bad loser or anything, but I'm getting tired."

"It's okay," I said, retying my ponytail. "Me, too."

I tossed the ball on the lawn and flopped down on the grass next to it.

Oliver sat down next to me. We were so close I could feel the heat off his body. So close our arms almost touched. And then he did it. He grabbed my hand.

We were holding hands again, but this time on my front lawn.

My boyfriend and I were holding hands on my front lawn!

This would be the perfect moment for Oliver to kiss me.

And look—here he was staring at me. Smiling and leaning closer like he wanted to kiss me. I could tell because he licked his lips. He even squeezed my hand tighter. I wondered if I should move closer to make things easier.

And would he peck me on the cheek or go right for my lips?

Would he cradle my face in his hands? I saw that in a movie once and it seemed cool, but maybe it would feel weird. Plus, we were both sweaty from the basketball game.

I should probably lean in so he could kiss me on the lips.

And as I had that thought, he leaned even closer.

Our lips were inches apart. I could feel his warm breath on my face and see each of his long eyelashes. Then suddenly I heard a loud rumbling and an all-too-familiar voice.

"Spazabelle and Oliver, sitting in a tree, k-i-s-s-i-n-g. First comes love. Then comes marriage. Then comes the baby in the baby carriage."

No no no! This is not how it's supposed to go.

Oliver pulled away and looked up.

Jackson was on the sidewalk, making out with his hand.

"Go away!" I shouted, pulling up some grass and throwing it at him.

Jackson laughed and continued on down the street.

I shook my head. "That dude is annoying!"

"I should probably go." Oliver stood up and brushed the grass off the bottom of his jeans.

"So soon?" I asked.

"I promised I'd help my mom in her garden," said Oliver. "She bought a bunch of new tulip bulbs for spring. We usually plant together."

"That's sweet." I blinked up at him and tried to tell him silently that this would be the perfect moment to kiss me.

But instead of leaning closer he took a step back and waved. "See you later," he called, and then jogged off down the street.

Later that night, Rachel called me. "I saw you outside the window. Looked like you and Oliver were pretty serious."

"Were you spying on me?" I asked.

"Of course not," said Rachel, seemingly insulted.

"Then why were you looking out the window?" I asked.

"I was looking for you and Oliver, since I figured you two would be saying good-bye and I wanted to see if, you know, if he'd finally kissed you."

"That's kind of the definition of spying," I pointed out.

"Okay, fine, I was spying, but I didn't see anything good. So tell me what happened," said Rachel.

"Nothing happened, thanks to your brother!" I said.

After I explained the entire Jackson-on-a-skateboard incident, Rachel sighed. "Oh man, that stinks! I'm so sorry. I should keep my brother locked up!"

"Is that an option?" I wondered, only half joking.

Suddenly my phone beeped. "Call waiting," I told Rachel. "I'd better get it."

"Okay, bye," she said.

"Hello?" I asked.

"So, did he kiss you?" Emma asked.

"No! But will you try and be a little more discreet? What if my mom had answered the phone?"

"You sound nothing like your mom," said Emma. "And why not?"

"Why don't I sound like my mom?" I asked.

"Very funny!" said Emma. "Why didn't he kiss you?"

I told her the whole awful story, and then I had to repeat it twice more when Claire and Yumi called to check in. I'm glad my friends are enthusiastic about my relationship, but it was hard having to relay the same news—or the same nonnews—four times in one night.

Once I finished, I fed Pepper dinner and then headed back upstairs to finish my homework.

Science was out of the way—good. But I had a book report due on Monday—bad. I'd chosen to read *I Know Why the Caged Bird Sings*, which was interesting but not exactly uplifting.

Now I had to write two pages on it. Our reports had to read like book reviews with three sections: (1) plot summary, (2) this is what the author did well, and (3) here's what the author could have improved on.

But instead of answering the questions about Maya Angelou, I found myself thinking of, and writing about, Oliver and me.

1. Plot summary: Oliver and Annabelle are boyfriend and girlfriend. They do fun things together, like play basketball and PlayStation hockey, and they do their homework together sometimes. Before they became an official couple, he even taught her how to play cricket. They are supposed to have their first kiss, but it hasn't yet happened. He also drew her portrait once, which sounds romantic but was also kind of awkward.

2. The best part about this novel is that Oliver and Annabelle have fun together, and it's fun reading about their romantic evenings out, laughing over pancakes and sharing frozen yogurt, etc.

3. The worst part of this book is the suspense. Will they ever kiss? How will it happen? When will it happen? Where will it happen? And why hasn't it happened yet?

It's a very frustrating situation.

chapter eighteen
birchwood's got talent

I finished my actual report and the rest of my homework on Saturday. That night, Emma had all of us sleep over. We gave each other mani-pedis and rewatched the first season of *Glee*.

At school the following week, Tobias ignored me for the most part and Oliver and I hung out twice after school, but we still did not kiss.

Then suddenly, before I knew it, talent show night had arrived. Sitting in the front row with the other judges, minutes before the show was to begin, I couldn't help but feel jittery—almost as if I myself were performing.

Of course, in a sense I was—being a judge was a huge responsibility. That's what Ms. Benson, Ms. Lerner, and Mr. Beller kept reminding us, anyway. And I believed them.

Right before the show began, Ms. Benson passed out our scorecards. Each act had a card with three categories written on it: (1) Originality, (2) Skill, and (3) Overall Entertainment Value. Next to each line, we had room to write our scores. She reminded us that five was the highest grade and zero was the lowest.

"Zero should be reserved for people who don't show up," said Ms. Benson. "And think carefully about fives. A five should only be awarded to acts that are absolutely flawless. And again, I'd like to remind you that you cannot give half scores because it'll make the final process too complicated."

"And," Mr. Benson added, "please make sure you are judging each act independently of your personal feelings about the performers. It doesn't matter if you see your best friend or your girlfriend or boyfriend or worst enemy or frenemy onstage. Everyone gets a fair shot. Deal?"

"Deal," I said, thinking it also didn't matter that three of the contestants had offered to take me out for frozen yogurt or that one had promised me a ride on a hot-air balloon. (Don't ask.)

"Deal," said Hugo.

"No deal," said Jackson.

"Excuse me?" asked Mr. Benson.

"Kidding," Jackson said, throwing up his hands. "Everyone gets a fair shot. I've got it."

"Good," said Mr. Beller. "And just so you know—a few acts have been canceled, so we only have twenty-five to get through. This is great news because it means we won't be here all night."

Ms. Benson walked onto the stage and welcomed everyone. Then she introduced the first act. It was Fred the baker.

After he walked onto the stage with a large tray of cooking supplies, he said, "Hello. I am going to demonstrate how to make a key lime pie." Then he adjusted his white chef's hat and tightened his apron strings. "So please follow closely."

"First we take flour and butter and a little salt and ice water for the pie crust," he said, adding the pre-measured ingredients into a bowl. "Then we mix it. And since I don't have electricity onstage, I prepared the finished pie dough at home." He showed us another bowl with a lump of dough inside. "The next step involves rolling out the dough."

He did just that, sprinkling flour on the table and a little bit on the floor, too.

Then he made the filling.

After going through some more steps and then showing us a completed and delicious-looking pie, he invited a random audience member up onstage for a taste test. She was an eighth-grade girl with curly black hair. "What's your name?" he asked.

"Josie," she replied. "And that pie looks delicious."

"Thank you, random audience member Josie," said Fred.

A few people in the audience laughed.

Then Hugo leaned close and whispered, "Josie isn't random. She's Fred's girlfriend."

"Oh," I said.

Josie tried the pie, proclaimed it delicious, and sat back down.

Then Fred took a bow and thanked everyone.

The lights dimmed and he cleaned up his act—literally. He stacked all the bowls and measuring cups and spoons and his roller and took them away.

As I held my pen over the scorecard I thought about what to do. Fred's act was impressive. But was it impressive enough for a perfect score? It was original—I'd give him that.

I gave him a four for originality, a four for skill, because he seemed to know what he was doing, and a three for overall entertainment, because it actually wasn't that much fun watching him measure and roll stuff out.

I passed my scores forward, feeling slightly weird in my role as judge. Especially since Fred had been supplying me with great dog biscuits for Pepper every other day. But I tried to put that out of my mind during the judging process, and I think I succeeded.

Next up was an eighth grader named Sophie, who did a gymnastics routine that involved walking on her hands, three handsprings, a backflip, and a front flip.

I gave her a three for originality, a five for skill, and a four for entertainment value.

Then came Didi, the girl who'd offered me a ride to school. She gift wrapped while blindfolded, which earned her a five for originality, a four for entertainment value, and a two for skill, because some of her presents actually came out pretty lumpy.

The more I scored my classmates, the easier the process became and the less I doubted myself. That is, until Taylor's group came on. It seems that she and her friends made up, because all four of them—Taylor, Nikki, Hannah, and Jesse—waltzed onto the stage wearing matching purple leotards, black tights, and silver sparkly leg warmers with pink ballet shoes. The lights dimmed. Someone turned on a strobe light, and then Lady Gaga's "Born This Way" boomed over the speakers.

Their moves were perfectly in sync.

And not only that—Taylor sang. Her voice sounded amazing, booming, powerful, and strong. I couldn't give her a low score simply because I didn't like her. I wasn't judging her personality. This was about her talent, and she had a lot. Not only Taylor, either. Her friends were talented, too. And I could tell they'd worked hard.

I gave them a five for entertainment value, a three for originality, and a five for skill.

Emma came up next, with four of her friends from honors English. I sat back, ready for a spelling bee, except the group surprised me. Rather than holding an actual spelling bee, they performed a song and dance from a musical called *The 25th Annual Putnam County Spelling Bee.*

They earned decent marks for entertainment value, even though they sang off-key.

Rachel pedaled onto the stage on her unicycle and managed to juggle while riding around in figure eights on stage. It was impressive! I had to give her high marks in all categories.

The string quartet performed a very nice ballad,

and I gave them high marks because their act was good, not because of any special favors. (Earlier this week the girl who'd complimented my hair band offered to do my homework for me, but of course, I'd declined.)

Then came my true test. Oliver came onstage carrying his lucky sketch pad under his arm and also a small folding easel. "Hi!" he said. "I'm Oliver Banks, and I'm going to pick three random people from the audience to draw. Do I have any volunteers?" he asked.

A few people raised their hands. Oliver chose an older man sitting near the front, a six-year-old girl who was probably someone's little sister, and Ms. Roberts, our science teacher.

Then he looked at his stopwatch and began drawing.

Oliver drew and drew and drew. The audience stared. While it was cool to see him create something from nothing, it took a long time. He probably should've talked about what he was doing or played some music or done something else to liven things up, except he didn't. It was simply Oliver onstage drawing.

Ms. Benson told him his time was up before he'd finished with the third drawing.

"Okay," said Oliver, seemingly flustered. "Thank you."

I stared at my scorecard, wondering what to do.

Oliver's act was original. I gave him a five for that. No one else in the entire school did anything close to drawing portraits in public. And attempting to do three in five minutes? It was ambitious, too. Oliver did have tons of skill, and I wanted to give him the highest mark in that category, as well. The two portraits he had finished? They were impressive.

But he hadn't accomplished what he'd set out to do: three finished portraits. That was a sticking point. I wished I could give him a three and a half, but since I couldn't, and it didn't seem fair to give him a four, I gave him a three.

As for the entertainment value? If I were honest with myself, and I had to be honest, his act wasn't that, well, entertaining. It was kind of . . . boring. Not that I'd ever say so. There was no need. I wasn't cruel. But I couldn't give him a high score.

I gave him a two, turned my card facedown, and passed it along.

Next came another lip-synching act. Then a couple performed a scene from *Romeo and Juliet*, and then there was another dance number. Next came a stand-up comedy routine, and then Yumi pitching. Two kids in a row did a rap, and the lyrics had no swear words.

Tobias's magic act was even better the second time around. He'd added a cool trick involving linking and unlinking large silver hoops that didn't seem to have any openings. He also brought out a smoke machine during his "sawing the stuffed lady in half" number.

It seemed strange to give Tobias—the most annoying guy I know—a better score than Oliver, whom I adore. But Tobias's act was awesome. He got a five for entertainment and skill and a four for originality.

When the show ended Ms. Lerner invited all of the performers onstage to take a bow. "Birchwood has so much talent!" she said. "This judging process has been tough. You are all winners—that much is clear—but we will announce the official winners in about ten minutes."

Ms. Benson led all of the judges into an office backstage so we could tally up the votes.

Hugo was sweating and his hair was messier than usual. Jackson's eyes narrowed in concentration as he watched Ms. Lerner and Mr. Beller add up points. None of us said a word.

After a few long minutes, Mr. Beller cleared his throat. "This is surprising," he said. "The first place prize goes to Tobias the magician. I don't think a sixth grader has ever won."

"His show was awesome," said Jackson. "Who came in second?"

"For second place we have a three-way tie," said Ms. Benson. "It's Sophie the gymnast; Ted, Gemma, Diego, and Jasper, the group who performed the scene from the *Pirates of the Caribbean*; and Rachel the unicycling juggler."

"Oh, man, my sister's never gonna let me live this down," said Jackson.

"Go, Rachel!" I said.

"And in third place we have Taylor, Jesse, Nikki, and Hannah performing 'Born This Way.'"

So that was it. Part of me had hoped that Oliver

would somehow place. Now I felt bad. But at least it was all over.

Of course, I still had to face everyone at the wrap party.

As soon as I walked in I saw Didi, the blindfolded gift wrapper. "Hey," I said. "You were awesome."

She looked at me, a blank expression on her face. "Do I know you?" she asked before turning her back on me.

"Um, apparently not," I said to her back, more amused than insulted.

I continued on through the crowd and ran into Fred the baker next.

"Thanks for the dog biscuits," I said. "Pepper loved them! And I've been craving key lime pie ever since your act. It was so cool."

"Although apparently not cool enough," said Fred before storming off.

I noticed the girl who gave me saltwater taffy last week, but as soon as I caught her eye, she looked away.

Oh, well. I guess I know who my real friends are. I found Emma, Claire, and Yumi huddled in a corner.

"Hi. Congrats, everyone!" I said.

"Hey, Annabelle. Great judging," said Yumi.

"So you're not upset that you lost?"

Yumi looked surprised. "I threw eight strikes out of ten. I did well but didn't deserve to win."

"And as much as I love my fashion line," said Claire,

tossing her pink feathered boa over her shoulder, "I am not surprised that the world isn't ready for my look."

"I loved your pieces," I said. "In fact, I'd love to commission a Twister raincoat."

"I'll think about it," said Claire.

Suddenly Rachel ran up to us. "Want to touch it?" she asked, holding up her ribbon to all of our faces.

"Rub it in, why don't you?" asked Yumi.

Rather than answer her, Rachel literally rubbed the ribbon on Yumi's arm.

"Cut it out!" she said. "That's my pitching arm!"

I laughed, happy and relaxed, relieved this was all over.

And then I felt someone tap me on the shoulder.

I turned around and saw Oliver.

"Hey, can we talk?" he asked.

My whole body filled with dread. Oliver had worked so hard on his act and he cared so much about his art. If all these virtual strangers snubbed me for not helping them win the talent show, what would my very own boyfriend do?

chapter nineteen
the grand finale

"Could you come outside with me?" he asked. "I need to show you something."

"Um, I don't really have time," I said. "My mom needs me at home because, um . . ."

Somehow I couldn't even think of an excuse.

"It'll just be a minute," said Oliver.

He grabbed my hand. I had no choice but to follow him. I assumed he was leading me outside so he could break up with me in private. Which I guess is decent, if there's anything decent about breaking up with your girlfriend because she didn't rig the talent show for you.

I wondered if I should tell him I'm sorry he didn't win. Because I was—I knew he'd worked hard on his act, but I had to be honest. His act simply wasn't good enough to place. And I'd worked hard to be fair and square.

Soon we were in front of his locker. No one else was around, and I had a feeling I knew what was coming.

"Look," I said. "You can break up with me if you want to, but just so you know, I have no regrets about how I voted in the talent show. You are an amazing artist, and I enjoyed watching you do those portraits, but I couldn't give you a high mark simply because you're my boyfriend. You didn't finish in time. I'm sorry if this makes me a bad girlfriend, but I don't think it does. I think it makes me honest, which is something you should appreciate."

Oliver stared at me for a second, squinty eyed and confused. "I'm not mad," he said.

"Then why are we here?" I asked.

Rather than answer me, he turned around, spun the combination on his locker, and swung open the door. Inside was a small easel, and on that small easel was a smaller portrait of me.

Oliver had drawn me! And he'd done an exquisite job. It looked like he'd used the sketch from IHOP and then embellished it, adding more details and color, too.

"I don't know what to say . . ."

"Do you hate it?" asked Oliver. His voice trembled. He was nervous.

"Are you kidding?" I asked. "I love it!"

I wrapped my arms around his neck and pulled him in for a spontaneous hug. He smelled sweet and spicy—like lemon soap and gingersnap cookies.

He hugged me back tightly.

"I'm so glad," he said. "I made it for you a while ago but was afraid to give it to you before the competition.

I didn't want you to think I was trying to bribe you or anything."

"I wouldn't have thought that," I said, pulling back so I could look him in the eye. "I know you too well."

"Annabelle, you're the best science lab partner ever."

I giggled. "I was just thinking the same thing about you," I said.

He smiled at me.

I smiled at him.

We were like statues, neither of us moving any closer.

And as I waited for him to kiss me, I realized something. I was sick and tired of waiting.

So I kissed him.

Yes, I did.

And guess what?

He kissed me back.

And it felt electric.

"Wow!" he whispered.

"Yeah," I repeated. "Me, too."

We laughed, and I kissed him again.

"Thank you," said Oliver. "I thought you'd never do that."

"Never?" I asked.

"Don't you know I've had a huge crush on you since school started, practically?"

"I didn't, actually. But I'm glad I do now. Does this mean you're not mad that you didn't win the talent show?"

"No," said Oliver. "Disappointed, because of course I wanted to win, but it's no big deal. Not when I have something better than first prize."

I put my hands on his shoulders, like we were slow dancing except we didn't need music. "What's better than first prize?" I asked, gazing into his beautiful green eyes.

"This," he said, kissing me again. "And knowing I have Annabelle Stevens for a girlfriend."

acknowledgments

Special thanks to the super-amazing Laura Langlie, and the Bloomsbury team: Michelle Nagler, Caroline Abbey, Cindy Loh, Nicole Gastonguay, Donna Mark, Alexei Esikoff, Vanessa Nuttry, Katy Hershberger, Bridget Hartzler, Beth Eller, and Linette Kim.

Major props to the Brooklyn Writer's Space for providing me with a wonderfully peaceful and almost waterbug-free place to work.

And love and thanks to my family, Leo, Lucy, Jim, and Aunt Blanche.